I0546974

****

DOUBLE-DIPPED
IN THE FIRE

(The Fire Series—Book Two)

****

A Novel by
Bestselling Author

Jeanetta Britt

This is a work of fiction.
The events described here are imaginary;
the settings and characters are fictitious and not intended to represent
specific places or persons, real or imagined.

Copyright © November 2018 by Jeanetta Britt

All rights reserved. No part of this book may be reproduced or
utilized in any form by any means, electronic or mechanical,
including photocopying, recording, or by any information storage or
retrieval system,
without permission in writing from the Publisher.

Inquiries should be addressed to J. Britt
(brittbooks@msn.com)
Twelve Stones Publishing LLC
P. O. Box 921, Eufaula, AL 36072-0921
www.jbrittbooks.com

Library of Congress Control Number: 2018906416
ISBN: 978-1-7327071-0-8

Printed in the United States
First Edition

Editor: Glorias G. Dixon
          Fairrene Carter-Frost
Cover: Michelle Stimpson

Scriptures from *The Holy Bible*
King James Version

To all my Sorors
...and to my Line Sisters...
Alpha Beta Chapter
Delta Sigma Theta Sorority, Inc.
Fisk University
Nashville, Tennessee
Δ Fifty Golden Years Δ
"Electrifying 29"
27-AB-68
Scholarship * Sisterhood * Service
Fisk Forever!
...and thanks for all the years of fellowship & fun...
Brothers & Sisters
of the
Divine Nine

Bent Twig

© Jeanetta Britt
www.jbrittbooks.com

Little twig
Meant
To grow straight and strong
Reach for the sky
But something went wrong.

Was it too much heat
Or too much rain
Too much pressure
Or too much pain?

There's only one reason
Why the little twig bends
The trials without
Reveal the weakness within.

Acknowledgments

All the lessons the Lord has taught me have involved pain and people. But I wouldn't trade any of them for all of the gold and silver in the world. I think the pain is intended to get our attention and put force behind the Word of God so we can finally see it, feel it and get it. And if we will repent, submit and receive it, our lives will grow in grace and we'll realize—by faith—that it's all been for our good. He can turn our mess into a mission; our madness into a testimony. So if my journey can help even one person see more clearly the love of Jesus Christ through their pain, all of these stories and poems that I've been blessed to write will not have been in vain.

But in any great endeavor, we all need help, support, advice and insight. Fortunately, God promises to give us "people for thy life" (Isaiah 43:4). For everything the Lord is teaching us, He's teaching someone else, too; and those are the things we need to learn from them. So—we all need each other—to help each other, teach each other, inspire each other—so that we might get to know Him better.

Many thanks to Glorias Dixon (*Fisk*) who always provides the litmus test for the stories and never fails to tell it like it is. There's nothing like a true, long-time friend who'll tell you the whole truth. And many thanks to Fairrene Frost (*OCBF*) who helps me stay well within the lines. And I can't say enough about Michelle Stimpson (*OCBF*)—faithful Christian author, educator, national bestseller, and artist extraordinaire—who through her insightful cover designs makes the stories 'pop'.

And many thanks to the readers and book clubs that insisted on a sequel to *Dipped in the Fire*—including, Tuskegee Alumnae Chapter's (DST-TAC) Book Club and the VP Book Club, Dallas. The vote was unanimous: *"D-O-U-G has just gotta get his!"* Well, here it is…and I hope you enjoy it!

Then there are the people in your life who have nothing at all to do with the writing process, but the testimony of their lives constantly encourages your own. Thank you Brother and Sister Posey for showing us all what love in action looks like for nearly 50 years. And Otis and Sylvia Banks for showing us what 61 years of marriage looks like when it's filled with truth, patience, and love. In a world filled with tragic stories, confusion and outright lies, lives well-lived inspire us all to keep-on-keeping-on in the Name of the Lord! Not to mention my spirited and spunky, 90+ year old, Aunt Bess, who always encourages us—both the young and the old—to be faithful, productive and passionate to do what it takes to "position yourself for greatness."

And, of course, many thanks go out to Pastor Tony Evans and Assistant Pastor Martin E. Hawkins—the dynamic duo—who provided a strong biblical foundation during my 25 years at Oak Cliff Bible Fellowship (*OCBF*) in Dallas, Texas. And, also, to the pastor of my home-church, Pastor L. R. Straw, of Greater Sardis First Missionary Baptist Church, who constantly reminds us that he's "established in his faith," and encourages all of us to stay anchored, as well. *It's all about You, Jesus!*

And a big thank you to all of my friends and family, who allow me to skip out of the circle for a beat, and then welcome me back with open arms. I love you.

And to my children and grandbabies—Jaxon and Shiloh—well, you know!

&

"When thou passest through the waters, I will be with thee;
and through the rivers, they shall not overflow thee:
when thou walkest through the fire, thou shalt not be burned,
neither shall the flame kindle upon thee."
~Isaiah 43:2

PROLOGUE
The Grand Wedding

After the major dust-up in the church parking lot at True Vine Ministries, Inc., Douglas Grand stumbled toward the church sanctuary, still shaking from his frightening ordeal. Fortunately, he had a back-up pair of trousers in his designer suit bag; albeit, they were somewhat rumpled after being dropped to the ground when he'd been forced to the gritty pavement to plead for his life.

"You alright?" his best man asked incredulously. "I saw that madman waving his gun in your face. I was the one who called the cops."

"Thanks, Chad," Douglas said, slapping his best man Chad Winchester on the back. Chad was not his first choice, but since Pastor Meadows had declined his request to marry him, he'd purposely not invited any of the deacons or finance committee members he'd worked with at the church over the years. So Chad, his personal assistant, would have to do. "Thanks again, Chad, but I'm okay," Douglas said, using his designer suit bag to conceal the condition of his soiled, pee-stained trousers.

"What was all that about, anyhow?" Chad pressed his boss for an answer. "Who was that fool? Was he trying to hold you up right here on the church grounds? I mean, really?"

"Well—" Douglas let out a long, deep sigh to steady his nerves. He hated having to explain his private affairs to underlings. "You see, that was Money...Money Mann. That's Melissa's only brother—"

"Oh-h, no!" Chad gasped. "So I guess this *Money-creature* holds you responsible for his sister's death, huh?"

"Something like that," Douglas said, as he regained his swagger. "But it's like I told him." He steamed. "And it's like I told the cops and all these other lunatics. I had nothing whatsoever to do with my wife's death. I wasn't even home the night Melissa died."

"I know, Douglas." Chad's bright green eyes flinched at his boss' rancor. "Calm down. We're all on your side."

"I know," Douglas said, taking it down a notch. "I know, and I thank all of you for joining me today on this joyous occasion when I make Willamina my bride." He chanced a twisted smile as a devious thought slid across his mind. *Finally...Pretty Miss Redd! The woman I swore to get next to...whether Melissa was alive or dead.*

"Well, we're just real happy to do it, Douglas." Chad schmoozed. "There's nothing you can do about the past, but thank God you're getting a fresh, new start today with Willamina."

"Right. God." Douglas nodded absently. "C'mon, Man. What're we waiting for?" He slapped his hands jubilantly. "Let's go get dressed. We've got a preacher to meet!"

****

And a preacher it was, but it wasn't Pastor Clarence Meadows, Senior Pastor of True Vine Ministries, Inc., one of Nashville's premier mega churches. Of course, he had been asked to perform the ceremony for Douglas and Willamina months in advance, but he'd opted to decline.

"I've already married Douglas Grand once to Melissa, when he as much as lied to me by leading me to believe that she was his first and only bride." Pastor Meadows had exclaimed to his wife, Candi, who also doubled as his church secretary, since she was the only one he really trusted. "And despite his *empire* and all his fame and money, Douglas is a sleazy character; and that's why I set him down from heading up the church's Finance Committee." Pastor Meadows grumbled. "And now that Melissa is dead, I'm not about to marry him to his third wife. Not me! That man changes wives like I change socks!" The pastor scrubbed away the sweat beads which had begun to form on his brown, bald dome, and his wife consoled him by nodding her agreement.

"Now, I'll admit," the pastor ranted on, "Willamina Redd is a member-in-good-standing here. She supports our Dipped in the Fire Ministries, and she's a real sweet woman with a great big singing talent. While Douglas, on the other hand, barely ever darkens the door anymore since he's no longer the Finance Chair—"

"But what did you expect?" Candi squeezed in. "From what I hear, he tells everyone who'll listen that he resigned to devote more time to his business expansion. And he'll never admit to anyone that you fired him because he didn't tell you about his first wife—"

"The predator! He probably only came through these doors so he could make the right connections and have his pick of the women-folk—"

"I wouldn't doubt it—"

"And for the life of me, I don't know what Willamina sees in Douglas Grand. I don't know if it's his good looks; or the fact that she's tops in country-western music, and he's a big-time promoter in the music industry. I don't know what it is." Pastor Meadows mused aloud. "But since the man's first wife, Wanza Johnson-Grand, is now a member here...and heads-up our Dipped in the Fire Ministries...it's just too messy for me to fool with." His bushy brows pinched together. "Just too messy—"

"But I really don't think you have to worry about Wanza and Willamina," Candi Meadows said sweetly. "I think Wanza has come to terms with the wedding since she and Willamina had already struck up a friendship before all this happened. And Willamina makes some serious donations to Dipped in the Fire in order to help the ladies and their children who find themselves in trouble."

"That might be so," Pastor Meadows rebutted, "but I still don't know how Wanza's gonna feel when her ex-husband and the father of her two boys marries Willamina Redd right here in her own church."

"I think she's l-o-n-g over D-o-u-g," Candi said, trying to mimic the sassy way Wanza would've said it. "But I do see your point, especially since Douglas divorced her to marry Melissa right here under our noses."

"Yes, but thinking back," Pastor Meadows consented, "it was a mixed-blessing for us all. Because that's what made Wanza start coming to True Vine in the first place—"

"You're right." Candi smiled fondly at the recollection. "And ever since the Lord saved her in this very church, she's been running for Jesus—"

"Indeed." Pastor Meadows nodded. "Wanza got saved here, and she went to work here, helping women just like herself…women who've been battered, or abused, or displaced—"

"And that's why I don't think Wanza and Willamina will let this marriage thing come between them," Candi said wisely. "They're both mature in their faith. They may not ever be *girlfriends*, but I think they'll continue to be sisters in Christ."

"That might be so." Pastor Meadows bellowed. "But I still hold Douglas at fault for this whole fiasco. Maybe poor Melissa would still be alive today if he'd treated her better. And I hear tell Douglas was going after Willamina before Melissa's dead body was cold in the ground—"

"Maybe even before that—"

"Say what?" Pastor Meadows groaned.

"Don't you remember?" Candi recalled. "Douglas started working up-close-and-personal with Willamina last year when they started preparing that mega concert for Fisk University's 2016 Sesquicentennial Celebration. Can you believe it…150 years of academic excellence—"

"How can I forget? Melissa dies in April, but Douglas and his mega concert still went off without a hitch in May—"

"And it was an unprecedented success—"

"Yes, and at first, I thought the black tie affair was a super idea for our beloved alma mater—"

"What with his satellite feeds and pay-per-view sites all over the world, Douglas made millions for himself and our HBCU…and he made a worldwide name for himself, too—"

"Yes, but when Douglas buried his poor wife in April and didn't skip a beat with that concert in May, it sent a cold shiver down my spine." Pastor Meadows' thick body quivered.

"And that's why I gave our two tickets to the custodian and his wife." Candi shook her head woefully. "I just couldn't do it."

"Yeah…and now he's planning to marry Willamina in October…and it's still 2016—"

"Just six months after Melissa's untimely death." Candi reiterated. "So either he was going hot and heavy after Willamina before Melissa died, or this has been the whirlwind courtship of the century."

"But for the life of me, I don't know why Douglas keeps changing wives." Pastor Meadows shook his head. "He can get the same thing from one that he can get from another—"

"Oh?" Candi raised her brows and shot her husband *the look*. Because she certainly didn't want him thinking that any other woman could take her place.

"Oh, you know what I mean." Pastor Meadows flushed. "I mean both Wanza and Melissa are…well, were…young, beautiful women—"

"Yes, but Miss Willamina Redd is young, beautiful…and wealthy…and white—"

"Oh, no!" Pastor Meadows hopped up from his chair like it had suddenly caught on fire. "You don't think that's it; do you…not the race card?" He scrubbed his brow. "That's certainly not what we teach here at True Vine. That's why we've been able to shepherd an interracial congregation over all these years, because the Bible expressly speaks against us having prejudice against any people. We are all brothers and sisters, not on the basis of our race, creed, or color, but on the basis of our *like precious faith* through the blood of Jesus Christ," the pastor said, borrowing one of his favorite quotes from the Apostle Peter.

"I know that." Candi smiled at his windy sermonette. "And that might work well within the confines of the four walls of the sanctuary, but you know that's not how the world operates."

"Granted." The pastor consented reluctantly, while steadily pacing a hole into the carpet.

"So what else could it be?" Candi surmised. "Maybe Douglas thinks that Willamina, because of her connections and her millions, can take him places that poor, black Wanza and Melissa could not. In his warped mind, they needed him; he didn't need them. But, now, he's planning to tap into some of that *white privilege* to boost his success—"

"But what makes you say that?"

"Well, look at his track record." Candi flashed her pretty brown, wise-woman eyes. "He went from promoting strictly blues, R&B and rap artists when he was with Wanza and Melissa. But, now, he's expanding into country; that new-age/millennial mess; and, of all things…zydeco—"

"Zydeco?"

"Yes, Honey…the New Orleans connection." Candi twinkled. "Douglas' greed has no bounds. He's getting his fingers into every pie, both in this country and abroad—"

"But how do you know all this?"

"I sit in your office, Pastor." Candi winked. "I hear all the gossip."

"But this just goes to prove my point." Pastor Meadows protested. "Douglas has already got an international music promotions empire. He's got his own money—"

"Yes, but don't you see?" Candi rebutted. "Willamina's got that much more. And from what I hear, she can make or break you in the music industry if she chooses to, especially in her country genre." Candi chuckled. "So her color and her clout probably fit quite neatly into Douglas' expansion schemes.

"For Douglas' sake, I sure hope you're wrong." Pastor Meadows reclaimed his seat and searched his wife's tender eyes. "Because the Bible is right, you know?"

"Yes." Candi sniffed sadly. "Nothing good can come from using people or lusting after fame and power—"

"Or taking advantage of women or wives to feather your own nest…be they rich or poor…black or white; it's just not a good life plan."

"And you've tried to tell Douglas this, too, but did he listen?" Candi said quietly.

"But if what you say is true, I really feel somewhat responsible since all of this is happening on my watch." Pastor Meadows placed his drooping head into his big, strong hands. "Is my teaching and preaching in vain—"

"Now, don't go there." Candi cautioned. "You had no way of knowing what was in Douglas' heart or his mind. You're responsible for giving the people God's word, but you are not responsible for their actions. That's the Lord's job."

"Granted." Pastor Meadows lifted his heavy head, blowing out a deep sigh. "But all the more reason I'm not going to preside over his wedding. Under the circumstances, I don't know if the Lord would be pleased. So I, for one, am not gonna do it. I am not going to marry Douglas Grand and Willamina Redd in this church."

"I understand," Candi Meadows said sweetly, happy to let her husband vent his frustrations. She held onto his big hands and branded his hot cheeks with her soothing kisses. "I think you're right, my dear husband, and you can count on me to relay your final decision to the happy couple."

Coincidently, Mrs. Wanza Johnson-Grand—active member of True Vine; Douglas Grand's first wife; and *friendly* to the bride-to-be—also declined the invitation to attend the upcoming celebrity shindig. *Naw, D-O-U-G...me and my boys ain't coming...not on your life!*

****

So the Assistant Pastor for Youth Outreach, Jotham Jones, was dubbed to do the honors. It was scraping the bottom of the barrel as far as Douglas was concerned, but he was left with no choice. Besides, Assistant Pastor Jones was tickled pink to perform the wedding vows for two of Nashville's most famous celebrities. What with Douglas Grand being the rising king of music promotions and Willamina Redd being the brightest star and dazzling darling of the country music set, he was literally puffed-up with pride to preside over the wedding of the century. And as Assistant Pastor Jones stood in front of the church, donned in his finest clerical robe, his expectation that this would be a grand occasion was in no wise underestimated.

The church was blanketed with bluebonnets and white roses, flown in fresh from Willamina's favorite florist in Dallas, Texas. In True Vine's cavernous sanctuary, they made a simple but elegant statement with a fragrance that floated you away. With no real family in attendance, Willamina chose one of her back-up singers to serve as her matron of honor. She was dressed in a long, flowing gown of golden silk threads, and her crown of long golden hair made her look like an angel.

When all of the illustrious guests—from famous hip-hop artists to country notables—had been seated by the white-gloved ushers, a gold satin carpet was rolled from the front door to where the groom and his best man were waiting. Well-wishers, with no invitations, flanked both sides of the balcony to take a peek at this celebrity event. With nearly 5,000 guests filling the sanctuary, it was fortunate that only the invited guests would be able to attend the upcoming reception.

Douglas and his best man, Chad, were both decked out in formal, grey tuxedos with tails and all the trimmings. Both of them were tall and brawn and made a very handsome pair. Douglas' deep chocolate face was framed by a head full of black, rippling waves, a well-trimmed moustache and brown eyes that glowed with wonder. By contrast, Chad's tanned face was devoid of facial hair, but it was complemented by a strong cleft chin and a crop of thick blonde hair, which set off his piercing green eyes.

As the bass guitar struck-up the first note of, "Here Comes the Bride", everyone stood erectly and gazed in reverent awe at the gorgeous bride who entered the sanctuary. Willamina's flawless, white skin and porcelain features were luminous, and her clear blue eyes glittered like a pair of limpid pools. Her flaming red hair was tied back in a white satin bow and artfully covered in a short, white veil. Her dress was sparkling white, and rightfully so since she'd refused to sleep with Douglas until their wedding night. And nobody missed the diamonds accentuating her regal neckline and her Dolly-Parton-like cleavage. The long, majestic train of her dress, studded with white roses and diamonds, seemed to come ablaze as she floated down the aisle to her waiting groom. She opted not to be escorted since her father was deceased, and her family from Cut-and-Shoot, Texas was not expected to arrive before the reception.

But no one noticed, because the aura of Miss Willamina Redd filled the room. She was the indisputable queen, and Douglas

Grand's 40-year old eyes nearly bulged out of their sockets at the realization that his dream—*Oh, to get a taste of Pretty Miss Redd*—had finally come true. This wealthy, well-connected woman; this country-western phenome; this young, ravishing beauty, nearly ten years his junior, would soon be his wife. *'Til death do us part...or 'til she's served my purpose...whichever comes first.*

CHAPTER 1
The Grand Reception

The Grand Ballroom in the Waldorf Astoria of Nashville was exquisitely appointed for the wedding reception, from the pair of elaborate golden chandeliers to the explosion of lilies and white roses that framed the expanse of the room. Silks and fine china, candelabras and Austrian lace, and the tinkle of crystal glasses set the tone for a splendid evening. Willamina Redd, the undeniable, new Queen of Country and Douglas Grand, the rising-star King of Music Promoters had tied the knot, and hundreds of beautiful people from all walks of life—the up-and-coming and the well-seasoned—had coveted an invitation to this elaborate affair.

Willamina had considered a sit-down dinner for her hundred or so guests, but she opted against it because she wanted to allow her diverse guest list—from rock stars to movie stars, from rap singers to country legends—the freedom to mix and mingle and get better acquainted with each other. Marrying Douglas, this handsome black man with a stable of young, spirited artists, and bringing them into her well-established country circles, she realized would require some delicate handling. But she had prayed about bringing their two worlds together, and she believed she was up for the challenge. Douglas had convinced her that their undying love would conquer all.

So tables were spread with elaborate portions of expertly-prepared international cuisine, which could tempt even the finickiest of palates. Ladies were lavishly dressed from diamonds to denim in an atmosphere of total acceptance. And the hum of light conversation, congenial laughter, and the flurry of well-wishes which filled the space were Willamina's reward for following the dictates of her heart. The eagerness with which these luminaries had set aside their differences to join the celebrated couple on the evening of their nuptials made for a very joyous occasion.

Seemingly from out of nowhere, Douglas' stockbroker, Les Evans, leaned in tight to relay a sensitive message. The words were few, but when he was done Douglas had to use his linen napkin to wipe the panic from his face before his bride could notice. He could feel the trickle of cold sweat tracing down the back of his tailor-made dress shirt. Determined to keep up appearances, however, Douglas encircled Willamina's hand in his and gave it a loving squeeze. And as leisurely as a king with his queen greets the loyal subjects of his kingdom, he strolled around the room greeting their illustrious guests. As far as Douglas was concerned, this wedding was having the desired effect and that alone had to be his focus. *By marrying Pretty Miss Redd, I'm expanding my empire to include all of her prestigious friends, too. And before this is over, they'll make me even richer; and I'll have every music genre under my control.*

Looming out of the corner of Douglas' eye, like a dark cloud descending over a West Texas plain, came five men approaching from the west side of the room. And as the delegation drew closer, the luminaries thronging the happy couple began peeling back like a tin roof caught up in the eye of a badlands twister.

"Cousin Jeb!" Willamina exclaimed by way of greeting when she spotted her family members lumbering in their direction.

The grizzly, mountain-of-a-man immediately grabbed her into a bear hug and danced her around the floor like a rag doll. "Willamina-Gal," he said, "you sho' do know how to put on a high-priced shindig!"

As soon as Willamina was able to extricate herself from his tight embrace, she smoothed down her form-fitting, red chiffon gown that she'd donned for the occasion; swung back her iconic red curls; stamped back into her five-inch, red-sole heels; and led them over to a wide-eyed Douglas. "Douglas," she said proudly, "this is my family; this here is Cousin Jeb and the boys." Her rich mountain twang seemed to seep back into play when she was around her kin. And with no further ado, Willamina began to introduce each one of them to Douglas in turn.

The boys? Douglas gritted his teeth as the introductions were made. *What-The-What?* The one closest to Cousin Jeb she introduced as Jo-Jo. He looked to Douglas like *too-close kin*—you know, the kind of critter that was on the front porch playing dueling banjos on the movie set of Deliverance. *Um-hum.* And for the life of him, Douglas couldn't quite figure out if the eyelashes over his vacant-looking eyes were white like an albinos, or simply just missing. The next in the lunatic line-up was Bubba-Dean-the-Bobble-Head, because no matter who was speaking or what was being said, his head was on swivel and bouncing up and down while his eyes flashed like a demented kewpie doll's. Then there was John-Earl, and Douglas couldn't quite be sure, but he could've sworn this shrimp-looking, hollow-cheeked fellow had one glass eye hiding out under his headful of scraggly hair. And last, but in no-wise least, there was Jabbo, who had a long, white beard that trickled down toward his navel. *And if this one ain't Methuselah's brother, I'll buy him!*

After the introductions, Douglas scratched his head in complete and utter bewilderment. *How could Pretty Miss Redd be a product of this gaggle of hillbilly misfits and po' white trash?* And to his complete amazement, Willamina pointed out ten or so more of the crazy-cousin brigade who were hanging out over on the far east wall. And he could tell right off that they were all members of the same clan. They were the gaggle of yay-hoos dressed in pressed overalls with shirts and ties of varying hues and hayseed in their hair at this very elegant, semi-formal affair. Douglas stabbed his tongue into his cheek to keep from howling out in pain. *And that's the problem with marriage…you never know what nuts are gonna fall off the family tree!*

That's when Cousin Jeb grabbed Douglas' hand like a vice grip and cranked it. "Well, how ya do?" he said. "Cousin Willamina didn't tell us you was a ni—"

"A n-ear perfect man." Willamina jumped in with both feet. "With a brilliant career, an exceptional future, and a real cute smile," she said, her eyes pleading with Douglas for mercy. Until she saw the beleaguered expression on her husband's face, she'd never once given any thought to his first meeting with her family. They were her kinfolk. They had always looked out for her. And to her, they were as right as rain.

"Naw," Cousin Jeb said, sizing Douglas up, "she didn't tell us none o' them-thar thangs, neither."

"Well, I do alright," Douglas said, uncoiling his fists and smoothing down his tail feathers before this quickly became an interracial incident.

"Well, you know, Cousin Willamina does alright for herself, too." Jeb's eyes dug into Douglas like twin spikes. "And, boy-howdy, we aim to keep it that way—"

"I don't know what you mean—" Douglas said, getting his back up before he could curb himself, because any sane person would've known that trying to talk to these yay-hoos was a lost cause.

"Well, I don't know if she told ya, but all o' Willamina's near kin done gone on to meet they reward—her daddy's gone, God rest his soul; her mamma; and every one o' her five brothers." Jeb finally managed to place his right hand over his heart after a couple of failed attempts to get past his bloated belly. "Don't know how it happened, but sometimes it just happens like that…in threes."

"In threes." John-Earl's glass eye glinted.

"So the responsibility of keeping our Willamina safe and sound has done fell to us cousins—the men what's left in her family." He quickly added. "Of course we got us some women-folk, but they don't count in matters such as these—"

"Matters?" Douglas squinted, trying to keep up with his jangling words and the stonewashed, expressionless faces on this supremely butkus band of crazies.

"I'm gon' tell you a little story, Doug," Cousin Jeb said in a jovial manner, and Bubba-Dean's head bobbled to the cadence of his snorts. "Can I call you Doug?" he said cordially, while behind his hooded eyelids he was examining the very measure of the man.

"No, I prefer Douglas," he quipped cockily.

"Well, D-o-u-g," Jeb continued, "we had a li'l cousin over in Ford County." He stopped abruptly and stared at Willamina. "I guess she told you that we live in Cut-and-Shoot, down nearby Houston, but we's mountain folk. All o' us old heads was born-n-bred in the Appalachians—up above Tennessee—that's where we find our roots; that's where we call home, and Ford County is up in the hills—"

"No." Douglas eyed his new wife as though she were an evil, two-headed clone. "Guess the subject just never came up—"

"But back to the story." Jeb grinned.

"Yeah, back to the story." John-Earl flapped.

"Well, our li'l cousin, cute li'l thang she was. Well, her husband commenced to beating on her for sport." Cousin Jeb's spine stiffened and his big belly flopped. "And we had told him from the first—jes like I'm telling you here and now—if'n ever you don't want her, don't hurt her, jes send her on back home."

"That's right. Send her on back home—"

"But she wasn't gon' tell us for fear o' what we might do to her no-count husband, but we got wind o' it anyhow."

"Yeah, we keeps our eyes peeled." Glass-eyed John-Earl carped.

"Well, to make a long story short." Jeb breathed in and packed on a crooked smile. "They ain't never found hide-nor-hair o' that joker since." He snapped his suspenders against his broad belly.

"Not hide-nor-hair—"

"Lots o' ways to have a real bad accident up in them-thar hills, and you'll never be heard of or seen again." Cousin Jeb glared at Douglas for emphasis. "And a real bad accident is subject to befall anybody what messes over our kinfolk. Am I making myself clear?"

"Cousin Jeb!" Willamina broke in. The not-so-subtle threat had certainly not been lost on Douglas, and his head looked like it was about to pop. Deep lines were carving into his chocolate forehead, and the dark waves framing his handsome face were squeezing his head like a grape. She knew her husband was used to dealing with salty executives and loud-mouthed clients, but she doubted if he'd ever come head-on with anything that vaguely resembled the hailstorm that was her family. "Cousin Jeb." Willamina repeated more jovially. "Have you tried some of that good corn liquor tucked away over there on that square table," she said, pointing them out and away from her husband. "Had it flown in from Houston just for you and the boys." She winked.

"Why, Willamina-Honey, you thinks o' everything." Jeb planted a sloppy kiss on her cheek. "C'mon, boys." He hitched up his hop-along and his side-kicks tripped over his heels to follow suit. "Let's go sample some o' that good-ole corn while the night's still young."

"They're a little rough around the edges," Willamina said quickly, as a way of explanation to her bewildered husband, "but their hearts are in the right place."

And what place might that be? Douglas granted his wife a shallow nod and a forced smile. His insides were sizzling, but he made it a practice never to speak before weighing all of his options. *Okay-Okay...this has been a wedding day to remember...first, Money—the fool with the gun; then my good-for-nothing stockbroker—the bad news bear; and now, these crazy, hillbilly lunatics—trying to pass themselves off as family. Nobody gets to threaten me at my own party...nobody! This is my marriage, and I'll do with it what I please! But, okay-okay, today they all get a pass. But Pretty Miss Redd had better make this a wedding night to remember...or I just might call this whole thing off!*

"Look, Darling," Douglas said, deflecting his flaming thoughts and Willamina's attention to the other side of the room. "Isn't that Marc A—? Yes, it is!" He waved at the Smooth Jazz notable. And as though nothing at all had transpired, he led his bride away to mingle with some of his future clients and their more suitable guests.

CHAPTER 2
The Grand Honeymoon

"Wife-y." Douglas pulled Willamina's naked body even closer as the sun dared peek its way into the Grand Bridal Suite at the Waldorf. "You have certainly given me a wedding night to remember," he said, nuzzling close to her ear.

"Husband-y, I'm so glad we waited." Willamina squeezed in even closer, flowing her sweet vanilla all over his rich dark chocolate. "And I must say it was certainly worth the wait."

"I've got something to tell you," Douglas said, placing a hot kiss on the dewy mound of her cleavage. "Because I never want us to have any secrets; I never want anything but truth to pass between us."

"Truth is all I'll ever need." Willamina turned up her chin toward her husband, and her red curls splayed across her white satin pillow.

"As much as I hate it," Douglas whispered, "I'm afraid we're going to have to postpone our honeymoon in Nice. There's just too much going on right now for me to break away and go to France—"

"I did sense you were a little tense at the reception." Willamina encircled him in a tender embrace. "Is this why?"

"Yes." Douglas groaned. "And—"

"And—"

"I wasn't going to tell you this. It was so embarrassing for the poor, wretched creature." Douglas admitted, thinking he'd probably be better served by telling her rather than having her find out some other way. "But I guess I should let you know…if nothing more than for your own protection. You never know what a maniac like Money Mann might do—"

"Melissa's brother?"

"Yes." Douglas nodded. "He showed up in the church parking lot before our wedding…waving a pistol—"

"What?!?" Willamina's body stiffened as if to shield her husband's bare chest. "Waving a pistol at you? But why? I don't understand?"

"He's an ex-jailbird and a maniac; that's why." Douglas tightened his embrace on his beloved. "But I don't think he's crazy enough to come after you. But you never know what a loser like Money might do—"

"But—"

"Oh, that's right; isn't it? You've never seen Money face to face; have you?"

"No."

"Then I'll make sure my security guy pulls up one of his mug shots so you can recognize him on sight…if he should ever come sniffing around you—"

"But—"

"I just want to protect you at all cost, Babe." Douglas pressed his point. "I don't ever want anything to happen to you, Willamina. You're my one-and-only."

"Ahh—" Willamina cooed on cue. "I'm glad you're looking out for me, Douglas, but I'm a big girl. And Money Mann, or a hundred Money Manns, don't scare me—"

"That's right." Douglas let out a rye chuckle. "I forgot. You're that tough li'l girl from Cut-and-Shoot, Texas, huh?"

"That…and a whole passel of other reasons." Willamina was reflecting on her family ties—her ferocious band of crazy cousins—but she didn't want to bring that subject up just now. She imagined her family ties might still be a sore topic with Douglas, and she didn't want to dampen his mood or his insatiable desire.

"Well, anyway," Douglas said, feathering his own nest, "you're my A-Number-One concern, Li'l Lady, and I always want you to know that. That's why I insisted on you signing that prenup."

"Oh no!" Willamina squeaked out a light snicker. "Please don't bring that up again—"

"But why?" Douglas matched her resistance with a forced chuckle of his own.

"I didn't need a prenup. I trust you, Husband."

"I know." Douglas schmoozed. *'Cause there ain't been a deal made I can't break...if I want to.* "But since you know I was married to those other women—Wanza and Melissa—I want you to feel very confident that all that is squarely behind me." Douglas placed a burning kiss on his wife's cheek. "I always want you to trust me and know that you're my one-and-only from here on out." *And besides, this prenup will open up the door to your heart...and your millions.*

"So...is that why you wrote the prenup to say, 'If you cheat, you'll give me half of all your worldly goods—'"

"And you get to pick which half." Douglas' chest swelled under her embrace. "I want you to be just that sure we're in this thing for life—"

"So then...why did you insist on including, 'If *I* cheat, you get half of all *my* worldly goods?'" Willamina snickered to make light of the ultra-serious look on Douglas' face.

"And *I* get to choose which half." Douglas tweaked her perky nose with a smile. "It's only fair." He teased. "Besides, the lawyers said the prenup wouldn't hold-up without the mutual clause—"

"Oh, I'm just kidding, Babe." Willamina circled his bare navel with the slightest touch of her slender index finger. "If having a prenup makes you happy, it makes me happy; because I'm right sure we're in this thang for life," Willamina drawled. She'd lived in the city long enough to file down the hard edges on her mountain twang, but it usually resurfaced when she was angry, teasing, or counting on the strength of her loyal family ties.

"So you're right sure, huh?" He tickled her sweet spot. "You really do trust ole-Douglas, huh?"

"With my life," Willamina replied without hesitation.

"Now, that's what I'm talking 'bout," Douglas said, as he rocked her slender body tightly against his strapping muscles.

"Just tell me you love me, Douglas." Willamina breathed deeply. "And that's enough for me—"

"I can do you one better than that." Douglas waffled. "I'm in this with you all the way…forever."

"So…we will go to Nice for our honeymoon later?" Willamina smiled.

"Yes, indeed-y." Douglas promised. "I knew you'd understand. I've gotta go to New Orleans tomorrow. It can't wait." He slowed and allowed his face to crumble. "And then there's that other matter—"

"Other matter?" Willamina swallowed the bait.

"Don't know if you noticed, but that imbecilic stockbroker of mine stopped by last night?"

"Les? Yes."

"Well—" Douglas resituated his body slightly away from his wife's. "It was bad news."

"Bad news?"

"The worst." Douglas moaned. "You know I've been trying to sign Ryhema. She's the darling of the millennial set, and she's bursting the charts and the markets wide open right now. They love her!"

"Yeah." Willamina sighed. "If you like that kind o' whiny, bad news song—"

"Not much different from country." Douglas reminded her.

"I'd be willing to debate you on that one, suh." Willamina thickened her twang. "But, anyhow, go 'head," she said.

"Well, Ryhema's been on a European tour, and we haven't been able to meet face to face—" Douglas stopped himself when he realized he was whining. "But to make a long story short, I've got to have her. She's a key piece to my empire. So I went after her full blast. I promised her the moon...front-ended lots o' cash. Well, anyhow, I dipped too deep into my cash reserves...right at the time I was taking my company public...and right before the stocks went on sale in the market—"

"And—" Willamina had a slight twinkle in her eye as she tried to hurry him along.

"And I hate to admit it." Douglas slowed. "But I got myself into some serious cash flow problems behind this Ryhema deal and—"

"And—"

"And...my broker was only able to access enough ready cash to buy up 30% of the company stock. My own company stock! I only have 30% of the voting shares! And the first Board of Director's meeting is fast approaching in December—"

"And you're afraid that with only 30% of the shares you won't be able to get enough votes to make yourself Chairman of the Board and Chief Executive Officer?"

"Yes!" Douglas' breath thickened. "Without at least 51% of the voting shares under my control, I can't be sure I'll have the votes to continue to head-up my own company. Can you imagine that? The company I've babied from the ground up...over this long, challenging decade...my own company...Star Music Promotions International, Inc. I've got all these hopes and dreams...but how will they be fulfilled...if I lose the right to run my own company!?!"

"Douglas, calm down, Babe." Willamina kissed his cheek gently. "I'm here, remember? I've got resources, too. And I'm on your side."

"I know." Douglas let her console him. This is the opportunity he'd been looking for in a marriage—a woman who could put some skin in the game. *A woman who can help me build my empire.* And her words of financial support were falling like music on his bruised ego. "And I appreciate that...more than you'll ever know...but it's not going to mean very much if I'm forced to go into that very first stockholder's meeting without the votes I need to maintain my position as head of my own company."

"I've got something for you," Willamina said almost gleefully.

"What?" Douglas said, baffled by her apparent excitement. "At a time like this—"

"I wanted to give you my wedding gift yesterday." She pushed up in their love nest to lay her head on his shoulder. "But it never seemed to be the right time."

"Gift?" Douglas turned her chin to face him squarely. "What gift?"

"You're not the only one in this family with sources or resources, for that matter." She giggled.

"But—"

"Just listen." She teased. "When my people found out from your people...and don't ask me how." She warned. "My stockbroker went into action and—" She reached into the drawer in the nightstand and pulled out a gold-embossed envelope with Douglas' name scrolled in sprawling calligraphy.

Douglas took the envelope from his wife's hand and opened it. His hoots of joy filled up the bridal suite. "Willamina! Baby!" He yelped. "Why? When? How did you know—"

"A woman never reveals her sources," she said coyly, "but I hope this will go a long way to putting your mind at ease...and letting you know just how much I love you—"

"Willamina Redd-Grand!" Douglas hooped. "You bought the other 21% voting shares that I so desperately needed! I've got my 51%! Whoo-hoo! How can I ever thank you—"

"Thank me?" Willamina glimmered. "I'm your wife, Silly…and don't you ever forget it."

"Oh, no, I never will. You can count on that!" Douglas took a closer look at the shares. "But Babe, they're all made out in your name—"

"Well, at such short notice, my people just didn't have time to get it done any other way—" Willamina cut off explaining. "But what's mine is yours; and what's yours is mine, right?"

"Right, Babe! Right!" Douglas' body stiffened involuntarily at the thought of not being in complete control, but he'd play along for now. "Besides, I can always count on you to vote my way, huh?"

"But of course," Willamina said, eyeing his burgeoning body part. "Seems like someone else is getting hard and happy, too, huh?" She giggled expectantly. "Do you think we need to work on that big issue as well?"

And without another word, Douglas pulled her close and drank in her kisses, her body, her sweat like he'd been in a starving land, and she'd become his milk and honey.

CHAPTER 3
The Grand Alliance

Around 2 a.m., Douglas Grand and the famous Nevus Brothers stumbled out of the Club Zydeco, on the corner of Bourbon and a street named Desire in the French Quarters. They'd been talking business, smoking Cuban cigars and throwing back shots since about 9 o'clock the previous night, and they were starting to get a little tipsy. Normally, Douglas didn't handle the grunt work of signing-up new talent himself. But he already had the stars of Zydeco on the hook, and he didn't want them to wiggle off because some bungling staffer couldn't understand their French-based Louisiana Creole lingo or hold his liquor. Douglas could handle both. And besides, he'd already set-up a gig for the Nevus Brothers in Japan, where they'd been going wild over the soulful sound in their famed karaoke bars, and he couldn't afford to lose face by having to back out now.

Ever since his record-shattering, mega concert to celebrate Fisk University's Sesquicentennial—150 years of excellence in higher education—Star Music Promotions International, Inc. had become a household word around the world. What with the pride of country music—Willie Nealy and Willamina Redd—as his star headliners, it had not only been Douglas' professional best to date, it had also launched him into multi-millionaire status. He'd already pulled together the best-of-the-best in Blues, R&B, Rock, Pop, Hip-Hop, Country, and now Zydeco under his management tent. Now, he had his sights set on Smooth Jazz, and after that, the sky was the limit.

The Nevus Brothers had parked on the other end of Bourbon Street, but Douglas had been unable to make the same arrangements. When he'd arrived, an impromptu parade of men in yellow tights and pink tutus, hosting rainbow-colored umbrellas over their heads, had been blocking the streets. *No place like the Big Easy...laissez les bon temps rouler!* So Douglas was forced to park on Desire, at the far end of the block. It was inconvenient, but this meeting was important. And Willamina and their honeymoon plans in France would have to wait until a date which coincided with his business travel plans. *But unlike Wanza and Melissa, with their sniveling ways and pouty lips, Pretty Miss Redd is a star...a consummate professional...and she's big enough to understand my needs. Hmph...couldn't have made a better choice!*

From out of nowhere, a man dressed in all black and a hoodie jumped out at Douglas from the shadows. Douglas was stunned. Speechless. It was totally unexpected, because the French Quarters had the reputation of being a safe place—even at 2 o'clock in the morning.

"Gimme yo wallet!" The hooded man growled. "Gimme that watch!" He demanded. "And make it snappy!" The robber jabbed the cold, grey steel of his gun deep into Douglas' right side.

"Careful. Careful." Douglas pleaded. "You can have whatever you want—"

"Sho' you right!" The man snarled indignantly. "Ain't no fun when the rabbit's got the gun—"

"See." Douglas whispered, in an attempt to tone-down the situation. "I'm putting my hand into my pocket. I'm giving you my wallet—"

"You got that right, Bubba!" The man rammed his gun tighter into Douglas' rib cage. "You ain't got no choice." He snatched the alligator wallet from his victim's trembling hands. "And gimme that watch, or I'll snatch yo arm out the socket!"

"Okay-okay." Douglas squeezed his Presidential Rolex off his wrist that was clammy from his frightful sweat. The watch retailed for over $30,000, and it wasn't easy giving it up. But in that tense moment, he was also glad he'd decided against wearing his platinum

Vacheron Constantin, which was a wedding present to himself and worth over $150,000.

"Know what?" the robber said as he grabbed the watch from Douglas and pushed it deep into his pocket. "I don't like you. I don't like yo kind. You one o' them snob-know-it-alls, and you thinks us li'l folk ain't nuttin' but the dirt under your high-priced shoes." The robber aimed the gun straight at Douglas' nose and cocked it. "And this world would be a better place with one less o' yo kind—"

But before the hooded mugger could pull the trigger, a tall, dark figure emerged from out of the shadows. He plunged his fist so deeply into the back of the would-be robber's kneecap that he howled in pain. And with one blow to his kidneys, the robber crashed to both knees, writhing in agony. The big guy finished him off with a one-fisted, back-handed blow to the right side of his head. Kicking the gun to the curb, he retrieved Douglas' stolen possessions; and while the robber lay unconscious, he whisked Douglas away from the scene.

"Where yo car be, Mon?" the big man said, while carefully handing Douglas his valuables.

"Over there." Douglas pointed, sucking for wind. It was happening too fast for him to take it all in.

"Come now." The big man wheeled him in the direction of his car, and they were down the block in a flash.

"Who are you?" Douglas chanced to ask when they finally got to his rented Mercedes. Under the antique street light, he finally noticed that his guardian had a giant bowie knife strapped on his waist and tied along his left thigh. His denim jeans strained against the thickness from his hams to his glutes. He wore a sweatshirt with cutoff sleeves, even in the cool night air, which revealed his bulging biceps.

"Essex," the big man replied in a deep, rolling voice. "Essex LaBrie. Who might you be, Mon?" The man not only stood at least 6 foot 5 inches tall, he was as thick and muscular as a giant sequoia tree. His face was dark, and smooth and uniquely handsome, like it had been chiseled by an ancient artisan out of a block of pure ebony. His jet black hair was bone straight and cropped close around his ears, signifying his Louisiana Creole roots.

"I'm Douglas Grand." He managed shakily, struggling to locate his car keys. "And I want to thank you…Essex…for what you did for me here tonight." Douglas stumbled over the admission. "You…you saved my life."

"I just happened along," Essex said nonchalantly. "Could have been anybody. We cannot have that kind of scum messing up NOLA's reputation. We be on the come-back trail, Mon; you know?" He grunted out the words and turned to walk away. "Bonne nuit."

"Good night?" Douglas persisted. "No-no. I'd like to do something to repay you." He was struggling to bring his breathing under control. "Tell me; what's your background? The way you handled yourself back there it must be something very special."

"Military. Retired." Essex grunted, shifting his rock-hard body to face him. He was a man of few words, especially when it came to talking about himself or his past.

"What branch of the service?" Douglas pressed.

"U. S. Navy Seals."

"What?" Douglas' chest started to re-inflate. "What division…or regiment…or whatever?" He hated not being in the know when it came to military matters.

"Top secret."

"Top secret? Wow!" Douglas was always impressed with the best. "You guys have a brilliant reputation. So what're you up to these days?"

"Jobs be hard to come by for the ex-military." Essex stared down at the tops of his boots—military issue. "When we are done fighting and seeing the bad things we see, there is no place for us in society. If you choose not to be a mercenary, you know how it be, Mon. And that is not the life for me."

"So what're you doing in the French Quarters?" Douglas queried. He imagined the military had done its best to make this man conform and extinguish his Creole accent. But vestiges of it still remained in the snatches of French phrases; the rhythmic cadence of his words; and in the way he avoided the use of contractions.

"Had a few jobs. Been the bouncer at a few clubs down here…off and on, you know."

"Well, in that case, I want you to come work for me." Douglas jumped at the chance. "I can always use a good man with a *particular set of skills*," he said in his best Liam Neeson voice, able to smile at his own brilliance for the first time since the ordeal began.

"What?" Essex shuffled quizzically. "And who might you be? I do not understand."

"Let's just say I own one of the biggest music promotion companies in the world, and I can always use good people around me," Douglas said proudly. "And besides, Man, I owe you…I owe you my life—"

"But me? I do not sing," Essex said bluntly. "What could I do for a mon like you?"

"You can be my…bodyguard-chauffeur," Douglas said, thinking on the fly. "Yeah, that's it. You can drive me around when I'm in Nashville—"

"Music City USA?" Essex parroted smartly.

"You know your stuff," Douglas said smugly. "Yep, you can drive for me and watch my back when I'm in Nashville…and maybe travel with me, too, from time to time. I go all over the world." Douglas preened. "And when you're not with me, you can drive for my wife, Willamina Redd. You know that name?"

"No." Essex admitted frankly.

"Well, you will when you get to Nashville, my brother." Douglas let out a rye chuckle. "She's the reigning Queen of Country."

"Oh," Essex said blankly.

"So whatcha think?" Douglas pressed. "You handle yourself like a good guy. You've got a brilliant background and undeniable skills. You need a job. Come work for me. I'll give you a nice salary and benefits…and I'll even put you up in a hotel until you can get on your feet." Douglas loved the art of the deal. He enjoyed pushing his opponent into the corner; and above all, he coveted the prize of being the undisputed winner. "So whatcha say?"

"But why you be needing a bodyguard, Mon?" Essex's beautiful black brow creased. "You look like a mon of means. I do not understand."

"Well, I am successful." Douglas boasted. "And as my empire grows, some people may get a li'l crazy around big money; you know how it is." Douglas slowed. "Speaking of which, there is this one guy…calls himself Money. Well, I've had a few run-ins with him already, and I don't want another. Got it?"

"So you want someone you can trust to watch yo six, Mon." Essex summed up the matter flatly. "Look out for your best interests when yo back is turned."

"Mine…and my wife's." Douglas added.

"Essex LaBrie. Music City USA. Active reconnaissance. Flanking yo six…Mizter and Miz G…like a true member of the Secret Service, heh?" He rolled the offer around in his head aloud. "Well, Mon, you got yo'self a bodyguard-chauffeur. When is it that I start?"

"Come see me in Nashville next week, and we'll make all the arrangements," Douglas said proudly. "And I'll give you all the dope on this Money-character, too."

"You have made yourself a deal, Mon." Essex shook Douglas' hand so firmly that he winced from the pressure of the big man's hand. "Give me your details, and next week, I will be there."

CHAPTER 4
The Grand Meeting

December 15th had finally rolled around—the date set for the first, long-awaited Shareholder's Meeting. Douglas could taste it. At 2 o'clock that afternoon, he would be voted in as the Chairman of the Board and Chief Executive Officer of his prized possession— Star Music Promotions International, Inc. He had made all of the arrangements well in advance. It was his decision not to bring any shareholders into his downtown offices—his private domain—in Printer's Alley. That would be far too personal. So he'd arranged to meet in the Grand Boardroom at Nashville's Waldorf Astoria. The room was equipped with a slick, 12-foot long mahogany table with 12 black leather, high-backed chairs.

He didn't expect many shareholders to RSVP to their letters of invitation, since he and Willamina held a combined 51% of the voting shares—his 30% and her 21%. There were only a few shareholders who held as much as 20%, and the majority of the remaining ones possessed even fewer than that. Most of them were expected to mail-in their votes to solidify his hand-picked slate of nine officers for the Board of Trustees, and his coveted title as Chairman and CEO. Nonetheless, Douglas didn't want to set the precedent for the few shareholders who might choose to attend to sit at the table, so he'd arranged for them to be seated along the wall in the matching side chairs.

Douglas had even been reluctant to make a seat at the table for Willamina with him and his nine *yes-men*; but since he counted on the shares that were styled in her name, he viewed the concession as a necessary evil—an added measure of protection. So he set himself at the head of the table; Willamina was at his right hand; Jim Jenkins, the corporate lawyer, was at his left; and the nine Board members filled the remaining chairs. Douglas saw the operation of the company as management's role, and he was management. It was his sole responsibility to set the agendas and conduct the meetings, and he didn't want any of the shareholders leaving there thinking otherwise.

Promptly at 1 p.m., Douglas took the gold penthouse elevator down 30 floors to the lobby of the swanky Opryland Towers. They didn't need to head-out to the meeting until 1:30, but Douglas was getting antsy, and it was his way of prompting Willamina to get a move on. He was dressed in a finely-appointed charcoal gray suit with a crisp, white shirt, set off by a magnificent silk tie and matching square. Paired with his shiny burgundy wingtips, he made a very striking figure.

He and Willamina had long since ditched their respective mansions on Legends Way and Peacock Place in the Brentwood Estates for a trendier lifestyle. Douglas had been more than happy to put the residence on the market that he'd shared with the dearly-departed Melissa. *Bye-Bye Wifey #2.* And he was equally delighted to get as far away as possible from big-mouthed Wanza and his boys. They still lived in the 5,000 sq. ft. Colonial monstrosity he'd saddled her with in the divorce, which sat at the other end of his block on Legends Way. *Bye-Bye Wifey #1.*

Since Willamina had owned Opryland Towers before they married, it was only natural they should assume the elegant living quarters on the penthouse floor. The exclusive address at 2000 Ryman Way was prized by locals and celebrities alike for its graceful presence and unique location—just a stone's throw from its namesake and the magnificent Gaylord Complex. Their move had put Willamina closer to her rehearsals at the Opry, and Douglas was now only 30 minutes away from his downtown offices; and more importantly, the Nashville International Airport.

Standing in the lobby door, Douglas gave himself a cocky half-smile as he surveyed his spit-shined-and-polished black Rolls Royce. It was waiting to whisk him and his bride away, courtesy of his new man, Essex LaBrie. But Douglas' smile widened into a grin when he recalled the first time Essex had ever laid eyes on Willamina.

****

A man of his word, Essex had flown to Nashville to meet Douglas a week to the day of their frightful chance meeting in the French Quarters. They'd made the arrangement for Douglas to drive the Rolls to the airport, so that Essex could drive away and get the hang of navigating the vehicle and the city.

"It was good of you to pick me up like this, Mizter G," Essex said, as the men pounded each other's backs in a strong, manly embrace.

"No worries," Douglas replied, as he took up his proper station in the rear passenger compartment of the Rolls. "Got to get you ready to meet my city."

"Where to from here?" Essex put the Rolls into gear.

"This baby is equipped with a navigation system, but I'll direct you today." Douglas offered. "You hungry?"

"No." Essex grunted. "I am prepared to take up my duties. Where to?"

"Take a right here to get on the freeway," Douglas said, while checking his phone messages. "And I'll direct you to True Vine Church. My wife's over there for a meeting or something. We'll pick her up and take her home, and then we're off to some important business."

When they arrived at True Vine, Willamina was waiting in the doorway with Candi Meadows, the pastor's wife, and a few of the office staff. Douglas directed Essex to park on the concrete drive a few feet from the building so everyone could get a real good look at him sitting in the power seat of his chauffeur-driven Rolls Royce. Douglas had not attended church since Pastor Meadows had snubbed him by not presiding over his wedding ceremony. Although, for reasons he could not fathom, Willamina had continued to be a church faithful. Douglas lowered the back window and gave them all a princess wave to feed their curiosity and fuel their jealousy. *Bet tongues will wag, now, huh? Who needs yo old Finance Committee...eat yo hearts out!*

When Willamina sauntered over to the waiting vehicle, Essex hopped out to open the rear door for her. Her back was turned to him initially, because she was still waving her goodbyes to her friends. But when she turned around, and he saw her full face and full figure, Essex nearly passed out. Her red hair was ablaze in the beams of fall sunlight; her skin was luminous without makeup and satiny smooth; and her bountiful bosom reigned over her slim waist and trim hips like the masthead on one of the legendary sailing vessels in his beloved New Orleans. The breadth of her beauty overwhelmed him, and as was his hot-blooded Creole way, he could barely contain his urge to grab her up; kiss her; and have his way with her. When he'd finally recovered his tongue, Essex spoke through a series of heavy, hot breaths. "Good afternoon, Miz G," he said, "I be yo new man...Essex...Essex LaBrie...yo new body...bodyguard...uhh... chauffeur."

Accustomed to having an immediate effect on men, Willamina had been smiling throughout his whole ordeal. She thought nothing of it. She knew it would pass. "And howdy to you, too, Essex," Willamina said, giving him a touch of her mountain drawl to set him at ease. She thought it a fair exchange for the amazing lilt of his French Creole tongue. "My husband, Douglas, has told me so many good things about you." She gave him a shallow embrace. "Welcome to our family!"

"Yes, ma'am," Essex stuttered, as he escorted her into the rear door. "Thank you, ma'am," he said, trying to hide his amorous feelings under a cloak of southern gentility.

But Douglas wasn't fooled; in fact, he was amused. A blind man could see Essex's raw attraction for his wife. *My man, Essex...got the hots for Pretty Miss Redd.* Douglas smiled to himself and filed away the juicy tidbit for future use. He thrived on exploiting the weaknesses of others. It was his strength. *Never know when it might come in handy. Hmm?*

****

When Willamina finally made her way to the waiting Rolls, for what seemed like an eternity to Douglas, he was anxious to get to the Shareholder's Meeting. They had just 30 minutes to get there. Essex quietly opened the door for Willamina, who was looking her radiant best, and ushered her in to meet her waiting husband. He rarely looked at Willamina head-on anymore for fear of becoming a blubbering piece of jelly in her presence. "Thank you, Essex" had become her patented response to his many acts of shy gallantry.

"Get us to the Waldorf." Douglas barked at Essex, as was his practice. "And make it snappy!"

"Yes, Boss." Essex roared up the engine. Douglas used the remote to close the tinted partition between themselves and Essex. But the passenger compartment was not completely soundproof, so the chauffeur could still distinguish their muffled voices.

"I think I've thought of everything for today, Sweetheart." Douglas kissed Willamina's cheek. "With my shares and the ones you gave me as a wedding present, I have the 51% voting shares I need. I'll be Chairman and CEO by the time this meeting's over."

"You're mighty cock sure of yourself, huh?" Willamina's eyes twinkled into a smile. "And I'm real happy for you, Babe."

"In fact, I'm so sure of myself." Douglas winked. "I'm moving on to my next conquest—"

"Oh?"

"Yep, these Smooth Jazz artists are a real tight knit group, alright. But I've been in talks with Marc, Peter, and Dave…independently of course…and if any one of the big dominoes falls, the rest are sure to topple over in my direction."

"Sounds like you're making progress," Willamina said encouragingly, but she was determined to stay in the moment since this was her first personal forage into the stock market. "But do you think there's any chance our stock will fall like a flatiron any time soon—"

"Not a chance." Douglas puffed out his chest. "I'm dedicated to solidifying our base and expanding our market share, Babe." He winked cockily. "That's what I do."

"But how does this vote thing work?" Willamina queried. "Do you think you'll have any opposition? Do you think any of the shareholders will come to the meeting and vote against you today?"

"Not many…if any." Douglas held onto her hand like she was the only woman in the world. "Most of them, who bother to vote at all, have already voted by phone or mail. But I have the lion's share of the votes, and no one can take that away from me. So when the tally is complete in my favor, I plan to have the staff bring in champagne flutes and some of those piping hot Big Hattye's chocolate chip cookies, the Nashville favorite. And I'll say to everyone, something like, 'Here's to the sweet smell of success!' Now, that oughta set 'em on their ear, and put 'em on notice that *I* rule Music City USA."

When Essex pulled up to the valet station, Douglas hopped out and headed for the hotel's gleaming revolving doors. Essex quietly opened the door for Willamina to exit. But by the time she'd joined her husband at the revolving door, Douglas had doubled back and was knocking on the passenger side window.

Essex lowered it promptly. "Yes, Mizter G?"

"This is a very big day for me." Douglas snapped. "Be on sharp watch. I do not want that *Money-Mann-character* anywhere near me today. No slip ups! Keep him off me! Understood?"

Douglas sailed off back to the hotel before he could hear his bodyguard-chauffeur's reply, "Yes, Boss." *That Money-guy surely put the fear of God into Mizter G.* But Douglas' hyper-vigilance gave Essex pause for concern. He had been feeling like there were eyes on him of late. Nothing he could pin down, but he'd had the eerie feeling, from time to time, of being watched—even followed. *Maybe…it be all these fat cats messing with my radar…or maybe…it be that sweet scent of Miz G…or maybe…I jez be slipping?* With that, Essex parked the car, re-checked the carry permit for his concealed Sig Sauer P229—the preferred firearm of Presidential bodyguards—and went upstairs to set-up a tightly-guarded command post at the Boardroom.

CHAPTER 5
The Mann Mission

Since he'd threatened Douglas Grand on his wedding day with a revolver in the parking lot of True Vine Ministries, Inc., Money had become a changed man. Gone was the cool, stingy-brimmed hat. He'd traded-in his short, dark locks for a simple college cut. And it seemed that some of his swagger had also been left behind on the black-and-white tiled floor of Big Larry's Barber Shop. All that remained were his bad-boy good looks, dominated by a pair of old-soul eyes that appeared to have seen more than one man should; his toothpick, squarely planted in his jaw; and the cool, dap step he couldn't ditch because of his bad right knee, injured during his high school football years.

Since Money had abandoned his affection for demon rum and dabbling in illegal pharmaceuticals, which for far too long had taken him places he never wanted to go, he'd filled out quite nicely, too. Not tall, but fit and sturdy; he was no longer that gaunt, aimless figure with the hair-trigger temper. He'd also taken to concealing the homemade, prison tats on his arms under long sleeves. But he couldn't cover the ones on his hands. They were there for all the world to see and judge him for his past. But the effort was a constant reminder of the changes he wanted to make in his life.

He'd also taken up reading his Bible every night, because never a day passed that he didn't hear the urgings of Mother Whatnot's haunting voice, "Get to know Jesus for yo'self, Baby." Never a day passed that his heart didn't wrench in agony over his beloved sister, Melissa—*my po' Missy*—and how he'd failed her so miserably by not protecting her from the likes of Douglas Grand. So when he'd finished his parole in Nashville, he made it his business to find a way to give back into the lives of other hurting women like Melissa.

It was a rainy day in December when Money met Wanza. She was holding the door open for him while he ushered in three, bedraggled women and their children under a lone umbrella. He went back and forth to the van he was driving for the Women's Services Center to be sure each one of his passengers remained safe, sound and dry. He'd volunteered to transport them from downtown Nashville, on Church Street near the Parthenon in Centennial Park, to the Brentwood suburb so that they could find shelter and healing at Dipped in the Fire Ministries. He felt it was the least he could do to make-up for his lifetime of mistakes.

Dipped in the Fire was housed in the old Family Life Center on the back side of True Vine's sprawling 50-acre campus. The facility had been converted into dormitory space for about 50 or so abused and/or displaced women and their children; meeting and office space; a cafeteria, as well as, play areas and an indoor kiddie pool that the children dearly loved. Since the facility was on church property, unwelcomed men who might come calling in the dead of night with mischief in their hearts were considered trespassing; and the police in the affluent Nashville suburb of Brentwood took great pride in hauling them off unceremoniously down to the clink.

"Where's Fred?" Wanza asked quizzically.

"He volunteers only Tuesdays and Thursdays, now." Money responded by way of explanation as he tapped the water from his umbrella and set it outside under the canopy. "I'm Mondays, Wednesdays and Fridays."

"And I'm Wanza Johnson-Grand," she said cutely, extending her hand to him along with an appropriate, professional smile.

Money bit his tongue for wanting to reply, *Uh-huh, I know.* But he remembered he'd only seen Wanza when he'd spied on her and her boys for Melissa's benefit, when she was going through one of her jealous periods, which was most of the time. But Wanza had never once seen him, not once. But this version of Wanza looked different to him somehow. *Maybe she's changed her hair or dropped a few pounds, but this is one-mo' fine looking woman, right here.*

When he realized he was gawking, he extended his right hand—the one covered in prison tats—and returned her firm handshake. "They call me Money…uhh…just Money." He didn't know if Wanza knew Melissa's maiden name was Mann—before she'd stolen her husband, Douglas, from under her nose at the church-house—but he wasn't about to take that chance.

"Well, okay, *Just-Money*." Wanza wise-cracked, as was her style. She may have set aside her colorful North Nashville projects' street slang while earning her hard-fought degree from Tennessee State University, but pity the fool who stirred up those smoldering embers. Given the right provocation, her words could still set a grown man's pants on fire. But Money had been correct in his assessment of Wanza's transformation. She'd ditched her outlandish wigs for her own natural curls that framed her nut brown face, which was not so much pretty as it was strong, and sensitive, and true. The kind of qualities a man like Douglas Grand needed in a wife when he was first starting out in business. And she'd gone from a size 20 to a size 14, and all the pounds had settled nicely in her trim waistline, her thick hips and her crowning feature—her smooth, curvy legs—which she flaunted by nearly always wearing skirts. But more importantly, she'd found her passion—using God's word, the Bible, as the basis for helping women and children find their way in this crazy, mixed-up world—and the joy and confidence it gave radiated throughout her total being.

"I'm sure Mrs. Lawson is glad to have you over there at the Center." Wanza's eyes flashed brightly as she acquainted Money with her mission. "They're one of our best partners, you know. They send us clients who're trying to make a fresh start. And we're here to offer these ladies and their children safe shelter, nourishing meals, and hope for a better future."

"And that's some mighty good work." Money nodded heartily, getting swept up in her enthusiasm.

"And Mrs. Lawson was telling me just the other day that she was getting woefully short on good staff and reliable volunteers—"

"I got myself another job in town to cover my expenses," Money babbled as he tended to do in the presence of stunningly beautiful women. Although he and Wanza were about the same age, crossing over into 40; somehow, Money looked older. Maybe, it was his years on lock-down that had been indelibly etched into his frame, or maybe it was the sadness and deep sense of guilt he felt every time he thought of *my po' Missy*, which was often; but whatever was weighing him down put a heaviness on his whole demeanor.

"Uhh…a job downtown?" Wanza struggled to make the connection.

"You see, by having a paying job, it gives me time to volunteer at the Center." Money explained. "It's my way of giving back…'cause these po' girls out here in these mean streets…they sho' be needing somebody to look out for 'em." His words were delivered with deep compassion and strong conviction. "And I'm sho' glad you're here to help 'em."

"Me, too, Money," Wanza said, leading him over to the reception desk. "But before you go, I want you to meet Yteesha—"

"Just Y." She carped back. "I keep telling Ms. Wanza to keep it simple." She smiled. Now, at 22, she was still thin, tall and trendy, but she'd traded the downtrodden look of a street urchin for that of an up-and-coming woman on the move. "And you must be Money?" she said. "Mrs. Lawson's secretary told me to expect you."

"Good to meet you." Money nodded like the cool dude he was. "Guess we'll be seeing lots of each other." Money couldn't put his finger on it, but something about Yteesha reminded him of his

Missy. Maybe it was her long, flowing hair, or her intelligent almond eyes; but whatever it was, it put this young lady way off limits.

"Sure thing." Y smarted. She'd come a long way since she'd stumbled into True Vine Church, pregnant, a baby in tow, and nothing but the clothes on her back. But her years with Wanza, who'd taken her in with lots of love and few questions, had been good years. She'd gotten her GED under Wanza's tutelage; and, now, the permanent reception job was allowing her to have dreams of owning her own home someday. But for the time being, she was thankful to be bringing up her children, Austin, age 4 and Teesha, age 2 with Wanza's sons, Derek, 13 and Donovan, 9, who acted more like their big brothers. And the arrangement was working out great, given the size of Wanza's spacious mansion; because when she had night meetings, Y could look out for all the children. And when Y wanted to go out wilding on the weekends, she was happy to entrust her two babies into Wanza's tender care. Wanza had only one hard-and-fast house rule: No men...*and no mo' babies.*

"Well, I'd better get on back fo' Mrs. Lawson misses me and shoots a gasket," Money drawled, chomping down on his toothpick and slapping his trick knee into gear. He spun for the door, but before reaching it he turned back to say, "It was very good to meet you, Wanza."

Wanza, somehow sensing his appreciation for her mission and the depth of his sincerity, granted him a brilliant smile. Her even teeth were sparkling white, and her smooth, thick lips circled them like they were happy for the privilege. "You, too, Money," she said. "Good to meet you, too."

And with that, Money's knees went weak, and his loins melted. *That is one-mo' good looking woman...but too good for the likes of me.*

CHAPTER 6
The Mann Mess

Money's eyes were bleary from the tears he'd been trying to hold back all day. It was nearing Christmas, and too many days of remembering his beloved Melissa had forced him back down memory lane. Leaving his job, his volunteer responsibilities, and his thoughts about Wanza behind, he jumped into his hoopty and made the trek back to where it all started. He returned to Knoxville for the weekend.

Money followed the trail of his old haunts. He drove by his home-house on Sycamore Street, and he reminisced over the days he and Melissa were the prized preacher's kids—*the PKs—the Partners-n-Krime—The Mighty Manns*—to one of the most celebrated pastors in Knoxville—Senior Pastor and First Lady Walter Mann. *Shucks, President Obama even visited our church that time he spoke at the University of Tennessee.* But even that happy memory was overshadowed by the lies, pretenses and secrets that had dominated their lives in that little house of horrors. *Lies that drove me to do some unspeakable things...and most likely killed my po' Missy.* The house had sold years before, and the landscaping had changed; but Money could still remember the way it had been—back then.

From there, Money drove by his old church—the infamous Faith Freewill of Knoxville. Many souls had been saved through those doors, and Money could only imagine how many more had been lost. He had brought the only suit he owned with the expressed intention of attending church that Sunday. Maybe, he'd get a chance to see some of the old faces, and certainly get the opportunity to hear the new pastor preach. He'd heard a lot of good things about Senior

Pastor and First Lady Strong, from Mother Whatnot and others, and he wanted the chance to hear the man first hand.

But he wouldn't. He couldn't. He couldn't possibly bring himself to darken the door of that church. He knew all he'd see was his daddy, Pastor Walter Mann, bellowing behind the pulpit; and his mother, First Lady Mann, sitting in her coveted position on the front row in fierce hat competition with her rival Sister Sistrunk, who always sat directly behind her. And he'd remember how he followed his daddy to that Sistrunk woman's house every Tuesday night, and how he'd peeked through her window one night and saw them— *And all my precious mother would do is take to her bed on Tuesday nights like nothing was happening so she could preserve her perfect family image and keep the church on lock-down.*

And Money would remember the deacons who only worked to get him out of jail the first time so that Pastor Mann's only son wouldn't be an embarrassment—to them. Or the time one of the deacons put his hands on— *Stop! Stop it!* Money sucked air pass the elephant that had taken up residence in the middle of his chest and drove on.

Next stop: Mother Whatnot's. Mother Whatnot had gone home to be with the Lord before Melissa's death, but he had always valued her wise counsel, her prayers and the concern she'd demonstrated for him. She had been the only one in the church's congregation that had ever shown him true Christian love. So it was only natural that he would be drawn to her house as though she were calling his name.

The last time he'd seen Mother Whatnot was after he'd gotten out of prison for the second time. She'd invited him over to her house to explain to him how his mother had really died while he was in prison. After learning the truth, Money had made it his business to stay out of Knoxville. And since Melissa had gotten him paroled to Nashville, he'd decided never to return home again.

In fact, Money didn't learn of Mother Whatnot's death until well after her funeral. And soon thereafter, he'd been picked up by the Nashville Police on a murder charge. But that's an ex-con's burden, especially if he's a black man. *The po-po gets us trapped into their system, and they don't ever wanna let us out. We get hassled for every unsolved crime. And that bogus murder charge is why I was on lockdown when Missy needed me the most. They wouldn't even let me out to go to her funeral. Uggh! And I'll never forgive myself!*

Expecting Mother Whatnot's old house to be vacant, with only the haunting memories of their relationship remaining, he'd planned to do no more than a quick drive by. When out of the corner of his eye, he sensed movement on the porch of her house, and he slowed. To his surprise there was someone standing there who appeared to be beckoning him to come over. Through Money's tired eyes, he tried to make it out to be Mother Whatnot, but it was not. It couldn't be. But the woman standing there, beckoning for him to stop vaguely resembled her. *Is it an angel? Nope. That woman's flapping her arms like a pigeon. That ain't no angel.*

So Money pulled over to the curb in front of Mother Whatnot's house and stopped. Slowly, he got out of his car and approached the woman who seemed to be waiting for him to join her on the porch. She carried herself differently from Mother Whatnot, but Money sensed some sort of kinship. "Good morning," he said, more out of good breeding than true feelings.

"Good morning," the woman chimed back very politely. "Please, come in."

Money climbed upon the porch hesitantly and offered her his hand. The woman gave it a warm squeeze, overlooking his tattoos. "I've been expecting you," she said with a smile.

"Huh?" Money was confused and all bets were off, now; he could no longer fake his amazement. "Expecting me?" He twirled his toothpick like a swizzle stick. "And who might you be, ma'am?"

"I'm Sister Mattie Whatnot," she said proudly as she offered him a seat on the porch. It was a cool day, but sunny enough for it not to be uncomfortable.

"Guess you're somehow related to Mother Whatnot, huh?" Money said stupidly.

"You've guessed rightly," the woman said in her elegant tone. "She is...or was...my only sister and my last living relative."

"Oh, I'm so sorry to hear that," Money said vaguely, unsure of what was appropriate. This woman's erectness and correctness was throwing him way off his game. She was a far cry from what he would normally expect when being invited on this porch. Mother Hattie Whatnot was a squat woman with a ragged mouth, a homely appearance and crippling *'authur-itis*, which carried a lingering whiff of liniment camouflaged under cheap perfume. *Pee-ew*! But her sister was in every respect the exact opposite—different as night and day. She was erect and stately with the bearing of a prep school governess. She was wearing a baby blue cardigan with a long, navy skirt and sensible pumps. And for every verb Mother Whatnot would've murdered, Sister Whatnot perfected it in the crispest of King's English.

"Thank you for your concern." Sister Whatnot sniffed. "May I offer you some lemonade...and some of my tea cakes? They're fresh out of the oven."

"Uhh...no, ma'am," Money said, perishing the thought. *Not if they taste anything like them nasty tea cakes of Mother Whatnot's. Yuck!* "But how do you know me, ma'am?" He inquired instead.

"Oh, that." Sister Whatnot added a light chuckle. "My dear sister left me a note that I was finally able to decipher." She smiled. "And it said to expect a young man to drop by at some time...a young man with Nashville or Davidson County license plates." Sister Whatnot's eyes sparkled. "So no doubt that would be you, my dear fellow. Am I correct? Aren't you Money...Money Mann?"

"Yes, ma'am." Money straightened. There was something about this lady that made you want to be on your best behavior. "I just thought I'd drive through my old neighborhood over the weekend. It's getting close to Christmas, you know—"

"Yes, this season can make us nostalgic…longing for the people and places we love…and it can be very therapeutic to return to one's home from time to time." Sister Whatnot smiled. "Knoxville is my home, as well, you know. I grew up here with Hattie." She stalled before sharing her full story, but she wanted to set this young man's mind at ease. "We were poor back then…dirt poor. Our mother was a single parent, but she was rarely around. Our daddy had left her high-and-dry for the sporting life, and I imagine our mother thought it was only fitting that she should follow suit. So most nights and weekends, you could find her at one of the local juke joints…plying her trade—"

"Huh?" The air caught in Money's throat. He would've never imagined that a woman of this quality could've come from such a dysfunctional upbringing.

"That's right." Mattie Whatnot continued. "My mother chose to be absent, but my sister did not." Her eyes twinkled at the remembrance. "Hattie dropped out of school early to make sure I had enough to eat, and we had a safe place to live. She went without so that I could have everything I needed to be successful…successful in school…successful in life. Hattie, or Mother Whatnot as you call her, made sure we went to Sunday School and church every Sunday, and that we had clean clothes to wear. Even if she had to stay up all Saturday night to get it done, Hattie made sure we were there. We never missed…and our mother never knew."

"That's quite some story" is all Money could manage.

"But that's not all," Sister Whatnot added. "When Hattie realized that my grades were going to get me a scholarship to college, she saved and scrimped and somehow—" Her eyes misted over at this point. "Somehow, Hattie was able to make sure I never wanted for anything while I was away at college. I attended Michigan State University undergraduate, and went on to get my Master's and Doctorate from The University of Michigan. I've been teaching and living in Ann Arbor ever since." She slowed. "I never had any intentions of ever coming back here, but Hattie made sure I'd have to make my pilgrimage upon her death—confront my past and reconnect with my present."

"Oh?"

"Yes." Sister Whatnot sniffed quietly. "My dear sister left me her house and all of her earthly belongings so I'd have no choice but to return here. Neither of us married, but we always had each other. And I'm thinking of retiring here…probably what Hattie had in mind." Sister Whatnot glimmered. "Wise woman, my sister—"

"Yes, indeed." Money cheered, feeling much more at ease. "Mother Whatnot was quite a woman!"

"Yes, she was." Sister Whatnot nodded. "And I'm so glad a young man like you was able to recognize it."

"She helped me so many times." Money admitted. "Times when I would've hurt somebody…or myself. She tried to keep me on the straight and narrow."

"And that is why she expected you to drop by at some point," Sister Whatnot said happily, attempting to lighten the mood. "She wanted us to have this conversation."

"What conversation?" Money said, clueless.

"I understand from Hattie that you accepted Jesus Christ as your Saviour at a young age; is that correct?"

"Yes, ma'am." Money was back on his guard again.

"And since that time you've had some troubles…committed some sins…like we all have; is that correct?"

"Yes, ma'am." Money squeezed down on his toothpick, not sure where this was heading.

"But Jesus Christ died to pay the price for *all* of your sins—past, present and future—because He loves you, Money; do you believe that?

"Yes, ma'am."

"So will you let them go, now, Money?"

"Huh?"

"Will you confess and release your past…and accept the love of Jesus for you, now?"

"Yes, ma'am." The tears Money had been fighting all day finally broke down into silent sobs. "I will." His tears flowed freely, carrying away his guilt and shame. "I do. I must."

Sister Whatnot excused herself to give Money privacy to pray. But when she returned to the porch, she squeezed an envelope into his trembling hands. "Hattie told me not to give this to you unless I was convinced you'd accepted the assurance of your salvation in the Lord," she said. "Hattie said, she always told you, 'Get to know Jesus for yo'self'. Because until you did, you wouldn't be ready for what's inside this envelope. But after our little chat today, Money, I believe you are ready."

"Yes, ma'am." Money tightened up on his toothpick and lifted his chin. "I am glad to know Jesus for myself. He is the only way I've made it this far…and I do believe He's gonna carry me on."

"Good, Son. Very good." Mattie Whatnot smiled through her tears. "Then I'm glad to place Mother Whatnot's letter in your capable hands where it belongs."

"Thank you, Sister Whatnot." Money snapped on his toothpick and stretched out his aching knee. "This has been some kind o' day." He took one dap step off the porch and turned to face his newfound friend. In that moment, Money understood Mother Whatnot's life so much better. Maybe her arthritis was caused by having too many manual jobs over the years; and her dental care was postponed because she was funneling all of her money toward her only sister's success. And just to think that him and all the kids had snickered at her behind her back, and the adults never respected her either. But she didn't care what people said, or how they slighted her because she was fulfilling her calling; and she knew God was on her side. She knew Jesus was her Saviour and heaven was her home. Her body was for the world to see and laugh at, but she lived on the inside where there was nobody but her and Jesus. *Ahh...and that's prob'ly the same freedom Mother Whatnot wanted for me. And that's the family resemblance! Them two sisters don't look nuttin' alike; they don't sound nuttin' alike; and they sho' ain't got much in common...but they're both rooted and grounded in the same faith... and they've just about figured out how to live in God's world.*

"Thanks, again, Sister Whatnot." Money waved as he drove away. "I'll be sure to read my letter when I get home."

"Be blessed, my Brother." Sister Whatnot said, returning the warmth of his affection. "God's speed!"

CHAPTER 7
The Mann Message

The curiosity of what Mother Whatnot had written in her note had grown to a fever's pitch as Money drove back from Knoxville to Nashville. He was tempted several times over the tortured miles to stop along the way and read it, but he convinced himself he needed to get off the road before he dared uncork what it contained. He didn't know if it would be damning or damaging, but he knew by its very nature it had to be explosive; and he couldn't chance reading it while driving. But by the time he entered his apartment, he couldn't wait a second longer. He ripped open the envelope and grabbed a seat. Unfortunately, for Money's tired eyes, Mother Whatnot wrote as cryptically as she spoke. *Pee-ew!* But he'd have to muddle through her bad language and penmanship to decipher her message. He must.

"Dear Money, if'n you is reading this, Son, it mean I done gone home to my great reward. And it also mean that you done met my sister, Mattie, and I's glad o' that. I wanted her to have a li'l talk wit ya and be sure you done got to know Jesus for yo'self. 'Cause you gon need Jesus for this one, Son. Now, that they's all gone—yo mama, yo daddy—*and my po' Missy*—I thought you might need to rid yo'self of that Mighty Mann Madness. It ain't no good for you no how. It can only hold you back from what God wants to do in yo life. And a wonderful life it's gon be, Son, if'n you let go and let God. So I reckon you's ready for this. At least, I sho hopes you is…

You see, when we was a growing up in the projects, all the girls in town was falling out over this one boy named Roscoe—Roscoe Lee Jones—and yo mama, she was one of 'em. Man-o-man, he was one good-looking fella; I tell ya. He was tall, but not too tall. He had a head full of slicked-back hair; a strong manner 'bout hisself; and a real cool stride, you know. And when he got dressed-up on Saturdays, he was all swanky-danky. And whatever he said to them girls, they snapped to it. I was too busy taking care o' me and my sister back then to fool wit them kind o' thangs, but I watched 'em all; and I remembers. And I believe that's why yo mama wouldn't let them Knoxville projects touch her none in the least, 'cause she didn't want nobody to remember 'bout her and Roscoe Lee Jones.

You know what they say—mama's baby; daddy's maybe. Don't know if yo daddy ever really know'd, but he shoulda cause o' the timing of yo birth. They hadn't been married no nine months when you was born. But everybody in the projects know'd, and they snickered 'bout it a long while before yo daddy and mamma got to be so prosperous. And then I guess, they just let it go, or forgot, or something. But yo daddy know'd for sho. Melissa was his'n, and maybe that's why he treated the two o' y'all so different.

But one night over in the projects, one o' them sorry-tail gals Roscoe had been messin' wit saw him with another woman, and she flipped out. They tell me she took out her switchblade and cut po Roscoe from his rooty to his tooty, and that joker died right there on the spot. It was terrible, just terrible, but that's how them kind o' thangs goes. And I guess, in a way, it must o' wiped the slate clean and let yo mama off the hook. *So many secrets. So many lies.*

Now, I wasn't gon never tell you none o' this til I was sho you'd got to know Jesus for yo'self. And I told my sister not to give you this note til y'all had a chance to talk about just that. So if'n you's reading this note, Money, I's rejoicing in heaven cause you finally knows that Jesus loves you jes like you is, Son. And His love be the only love that ever really matters. So whether yo name is Mann or Jones don't matter a hill o' beans. What matter is yo name is writ down up here in the Lamb's Book o' Life. And since you've trusted Jesus Christ as yo Saviour and Lord, you oughta be shouting, too, cause it sho'nuff is! You gonna have a beautiful life, Money, if'n you trust God; be honest wit Him and yo'self; and let Him lead you all the way home.

Gotta go now…my hands is startin' to ache. I loves you, Son, but Jesus loves you best. See you soon in heaven…Mother Whatnot."

In a flash, the totality of Money's life became so clear to him it was almost audible—like the sound of cylinders falling into place to open a locked bank vault. The missing pieces of his life had finally clicked; the vault was now open, and he was finally free. *So that's why Walter Mann hated me so, and my own mother pushed me to the margins. It was always about them; it was never about me. And that's why my po' Missy could never be like me. She was too much like her own daddy…weak.*

At long last, Money could feel the tall, unattainable letters in *The Mighty Mann* moniker crumbling down at his feet. Trying to live up to them over the years had been a millstone around his neck, drowning him in feelings of failure, incompetence and despair. *But at long last, I'm free…I am finally free…to be just me…just Money. Praise You, Jesus! And thank you, thank you…Sweet Mother Whatnot!*

CHAPTER 8
The Grand Lust

As it turns out, Douglas Grand had an important meeting, too, right after the holidays. As the New Year rolled in, it was finally time for him to meet Ryhema, face to face. His lust to manage her skyrocketing career had made him take his eye off the ball, and it had almost cost him the reigning seat at his own company's table. *Thank God for Pretty Miss Redd. She beat me to the punch and bought-up those voting shares, or else it could've been a disaster! But that's what makes her a valuable asset to me...besides making me the envy of every red-blooded man in the industry. Ha!*

When Ryhema entered Douglas' lavish office for their first face-to-face, he was seated behind his massive, chrome desk, which was surrounded by a growing number of platinum records on his vanity walls. But if he'd been a cartoon character at that moment, his eyes would've popped out of their sockets and crawled along the floor to lap-up this nymph-like creature like she was a bowl of warm milk. Her headshots, press photos, YouTube posts, and posters had not prepared Douglas for this. *WOW! She is drop-dead gorgeous! No wonder her fans go ga-ga over her. Under the stage lights, she must look like a shimmering goddess.*

Ryhema had tossed her black sable jacket on one of the red side chairs as she entered. She was long, thin and slinky, wearing black leather leggings that ended at the tops of her red leather ankle boots, which sported black tassels in the back that draped over her five-inch heels. Her yellow silk, see-through blouse revealed the wealth of her dewy-soft, brown sugar skin and a red lace bra that peeked from underneath. Her hair was big and natural, like a magnificent crown of waves and curls, and her narrow face was framed by her expertly arched brows and thick dark lashes. The hazel eyes that took cover under those lashes were as bright and sharp as headlights on a foggy night.

"Come in. Come in." Douglas sputtered as he rounded his desk to greet her. This was totally out of character for him because he normally kept his seat to maintain the upper hand in any negotiations with his clients. "May I get you something…to eat or drink?" Douglas extended his hand and for one awkward moment Ryhema hesitated. But when she returned his gesture, Douglas whispered to his assistant, Chad, who'd been standing at the ready, "You can go now and bring in Option A." Douglas wanted to take this opportunity to be alone with Ryhema.

"Please, take a seat," Douglas said, offering Ryhema one of his red and black desk chairs as he returned to take his seat behind his desk.

"Thank you." Ryhema finally spoke. Her voice was as soft and sweet as a summer's breeze with the hint of jasmine and honeysuckle, which wafted from her costly perfume. "I understand our lawyers need me to sign some final papers."

"Yes" was all Douglas could manage. His eyes were glued to the red lace bra, and the single thought captivating his mind was what it would be like to remove it, one strap at a time.

"Did you get the final changes my lawyer recommended and have they been incorporated?" Ryhema said, all business. "I'm on my way to Manhattan to visit my family, and I need to get this done quickly and be on my way."

"No worries." Douglas managed to put some bass back into his sexy voice. Option B would've cost him far less money, but he dared not cheat a star of her caliber. Elsewise, his name would be mud, and he'd become a pariah in the industry. "We'll get this done and have you out of here as soon as possible. How was your flight from Denver?"

"Predictable," Ryhema said bluntly. "But your driver, Essex, was a refreshing escape from the norm."

"Essex?" Douglas felt himself getting warm around his three-hundred dollar shirt collar.

"Yes." Ryhema smiled sweetly. "He has a very unusual accent, but he's totally efficient…and doesn't talk too much—"

"Good." Douglas reasserted himself, perishing the thought that Essex could ever beat his time with this lovely lady. "That's what I pay him for."

"So…where're the papers?" Ryhema shifted.

"Chad is seeing to the final changes, and he'll have them in here in just a moment—"

"Final changes?" Ryhema's hazel eyes beamed. "Is there a problem?"

"No. No problem." Douglas was in full form again, and his voice dipped down into its lowest registers. Her seemingly absence of interest in him made him all the more hot. Most of the women who entered his doors were just itching to get to know him better. "It's just…your lawyer included some clauses that I'd questioned…but now that I've seen you in person—"

"The clauses concerning the royalties?"

"Yes." Douglas' sexy voice crooned. "But now that I've met you face to face…my reservations have been…let's just say…put to bed."

"Good," Ryhema said, lowering her lashes and folding her arms across her breasts when she picked up on his double meaning. All of a sudden, she felt very naked.

When the last of the papers had been signed, Douglas escorted Ryhema back to his black Rolls Royce where Essex was waiting. "Good evening, Mizter G," he intoned.

"Good evening, Essex," Douglas said in a manner that left no doubt who was in charge. "I want you to take extra-special care of my very special client," he said, opening the rear door to escort Ryhema into the vehicle. In the process, he explored the full extent of her arm with his hot hands. And he took great pleasure in the fact that she did not resist him. "Make sure everything runs smoothly for her flight to New York," he said in a very possessive tone.

"Sure thing, Boss." Essex provided a snappy reply, satisfying Douglas' need to be the alpha dog. *But what have we here, Mon?* Essex had never known Douglas to escort one of his clients to his waiting car. That was usually Chad's thankless task. Of course, Essex had sized-up Ryhema on their way in from the airport. She was pretty, no doubt. *A li'l piece o' leather…well put together…but this gurrl be no more than 25…just one size up from jail bait.* And in his mind she didn't hold a candle to Douglas' wife. Willamina's flaming red hair, her brilliant smile, and her bigger than life personality lit up the whole vehicle every time he had the pleasure of driving her. *Now, that Miz G, she be fine. She's a full-blooded woman with a li'l meat on her bones…in all the necessary places.*

CHAPTER 9

The Mann Desire

After reading and re-reading Mother Whatnot's letter, Money had a new pep in his step. He was accepted in Jesus Christ, and he was convinced that no one walking on the face of God's green earth was any greater than himself. As usual, he was very courteous to the women and children that he hauled to and fro in the van from the Women's Services Center to Dipped in the Fire, but on this beautiful spring day he had an added whistle, too.

"You seem awful happy." The big girl in the back of the van with no children remarked.

"Because I am," Money replied. "Why? Ain't you?"

"Man, there ain't nuttin' in this world to be happy about." The young woman snarled and set her moon-pie face toward the window.

When they reached their destination, Money helped the ladies and their children off the van, and they were greeted by Wanza who was wearing her usual welcoming smile and a cute red-and-white skirt to celebrate the first day of spring. "Good morning," she said, time after time.

When the last person was off the van, Money sauntered over to Wanza and greeted her. "Good morning, yo'self," he said smartly. "I was wondering if maybe you'd like to go with me to get a coffee sometime...or maybe even lunch?"

"Good morning, Money," Wanza answered primly. "I don't think that would be possible," she said. "I believe in keeping everything strictly professional amongst us co-workers."

"I understand." Money resituated his toothpick with a snap. The coolness of the remark had stung him, but he didn't falter. He'd prepared himself for her rejection. After all, who was he to such a fine woman? "But I want you to have this," Money said, squeezing his cellphone number into her hand behind a warm handshake. "In case you should ever need ole-Money." He gave her a crooked, bad-boy smile, and the look that passed between them could've started a fire in the coldest of hearts. And, then, Money was gone.

"But—" Wanza stammered after him. The warm touch of Money's hand had begun to thaw the icy glacier that had been growing in her veins. No man had touched her since Douglas Grand. It had been over three years, and somewhere deep inside, she'd sworn to herself that no man ever would. Absently, she pushed Money's number into her skirt pocket. She'd discard it later.

Wanza's head swung around when she heard a ruckus coming from the reception desk. Yteesha was having it out with one of the new clients. "That's why you're here in the first place...your loud mouth and your uncooperative spirit!" She heard Y say.

"I told you; I don't have to tell you my name. You can just call me Z-Pac!" It was the same big girl with no children that had been sitting in the back of the van, trying to rain on Money's parade.

"I need your Christian name for the forms." Y insisted.

"Christian name? Christian name!" Z-Pac yelled. "I ain't no Christian!"

Wanza stepped in quickly to soothe the ruffled feathers, but she expected this one—with her big mouth and old-style dookie braids to match—would be a troublemaker when they had their Orientation Meeting later that evening.

****

"Good evening, Ladies," Wanza said with a brilliant smile when everyone had assembled for that evening's Orientation Meeting. "I'm Wanza Johnson-Grand, and we're all here this evening to get better acquainted. We're all wearing name tags, but it might help if we swing around the room and let everyone give their name and their children's names." She giggled to lighten the mood. "And if you can remember, let us have your roommates' names, as well." There were nearly 30 women in the session, and Wanza took the time to listen to each one, until a heated discussion broke out.

"I'm Z-Pac…don't ever try calling me Zenobia Packston 'cause I ain't gonna answer. And I ain't got no kids—"

"Then why're you here?" A young woman on the back row with bright red extensions hanging below her waist snapped.

"I'm here 'cause I'm just like you, Trick…used and confused—"

"Hold on, now!" Wanza stepped in. "If we're going to live together, we must learn to be respectful of each other—"

"Fat chance of that!" A scrawny dyed-blond with six-inch lashes sparked. "Especially, with the likes of Z-Pac around—"

"I just call it like I see it." Z-Pac defended. "If that blows up yo skirt, then tuff!"

"So whatcha tryna say, Gurrl?" Another young lady with Chinese lettering trailing down the side of her right thigh intoned.

"I'm just sayin' no matter the details, we're all here for the same reason." Z-Pac snapped back.

"And what reason is that?" A young lady with lime-green, dragon-lady nails raised her hand.

"We let these men run in and out of our lives…just for kicks…like we're some kind o' theme park…ferris wheel…some flavor of the month club…and we be having babies behind all this madness—"

"Speaking of which!" One of the mothers in frayed skin-tight jeans bristled. "Where's yo baby?"

"I had a man." Z-Pac's voice dropped. The name, *Ishmael,* was inked in red across her heavy bosom, and a *Popeye* tattoo was etched on her chunky forearm. "We had a baby…but my baby died. And that man didn't even show up at the funeral. He was too busy *kickin-it* with his side-chick who he also had a baby by…same age as mine. But her baby lived and mine died." She sniffed back her pain. "But no worries…he ain't with that other chick no mo' neither…he done moved on. And, now, he's kickin-it with some other po' dumb trick. But it'll never happen to me again…not ever. I don't need no man's hands all over me. I can do bad all by myself—"

"Yeah…and by yo'self is how you're gonna be!" The scrawny dyed blonde with the six-inch lashes fumed.

"Let me stop you right here, Ladies" Wanza reasserted herself. "We may not all agree with her delivery, but I think Z-Pac has made some valid points tonight," she said amid a drone of loud grumbles. "The Women's Services Center is here to help you with job training and job placement so you can make a better living for you and your children. But Dipped in the Fire Ministries is here to help you build a future and a life." Wanza pressed her point. "We provide safe shelter and nutritious meals while you're getting back on your feet, but we also want to help you learn how to form new relationships with clear boundaries. We want you and your children to be protected and to know what you can expect. This will give you a viable alternative and help you break the cycle on just *kickin-it*. I think that's what Z-Pac is trying to say—"

"I hear tell you was married once yo'self, Ms. Wanza." One of the young ladies rocked her neck to the side. "And now you're divorced. So what's the difference between getting married and kickin-it? A piece o' paper can't make nobody love ya. A piece o' paper can't make nobody stay—"

"No, it can't." Wanza sputtered, somewhat shaken by the stark revelation. "As it turns out, I was killing off pieces of my soul trying to hold onto a man who didn't love me…putting up with stuff I didn't like…trying to overlook things I didn't believe in. And the day he left me was the day I got free—"

"See; I told ya—"

"But that *piece-o'-paper*, as you call it, *can* dictate terms." Wanza defended her position. "If a married man wants out, it's gonna cost him; and he knows that going in. That piece of paper can set clear boundaries…define roles and responsibilities. While I was married, I had expectations; and when my husband refused to live up to his end of the bargain, I had legal redress." Wanza tried to rein in her emotions when she felt her 'hood coming on. "I get alimony. I get child support. My children have a set time they expect to see their daddy. And most of all, I have order in my home…and it takes order to raise your children and pursue your dreams—"

"Yeah!" Z-Pac bubbled over. "And what you and yo kids got, Trick? Food stamps…Section 8 housing…no last names—"

"Now, hold it!" Wanza jumped back in, resuming her professional demeanor. "We're having a good discussion here, but we have to be respectful of each other's views so we can learn—"

"And what we got?" Z-Pac couldn't wait to jump back in. "Tore-up relationships…dudes running in and out o' our lives like the Indy 500. They ain't saying whether they in or they out. They're just passing thru…*kickin-it*—"

"And who suffers?" Another young lady tacked on. "We do…and our kids…that's who—"

"They have all the fun, and we have all the babies!"

"And the guys don't stick around long enough to see the mess they make—"

"'Cause they don't care!"

The ladies were on a roll, now. The heat in the room was rising like a steam cloud as each woman held fiercely to her position.

"As long as they can get at the *cookie*, that's all they really want—"

"Yeah, these dudes don't wanna get caught up in no labels, like married or single. Long as they can hit it and quit it…they're cool with that—"

"But why would a man sleep with you if he don't wanna marry you—"

63

"For kicks, Girl…why you think they call it *kickin-it*?"

"Yeah, and ain't y'all tired of jumpin' from man to man and bed to bed?" Z-Pac jumped back in. "Ain't that gettin'a li'l old?"

"Gurrl, you just gotta be strong in this world—"

"Yeah, these guys want us to think we're being strong so they can keep on treating us the way they do!"

"But some o' them are good dads—"

"Gurrl, you can't be a good dad when you ain't never around me and yo baby."

"You can be a good absentee dad—"

"You can send that cheese on time—"

"But that doesn't make you a good dad—"

"And we make it so-o easy for 'em—"

"This one dude told me, 'Gurrl, I can have sex when I can't eat!'"

"But don't you see?" Z-Pac shouted. "If you're not having sex with a man, you can just move on to the next one if you find out he ain't the right dude for you—"

"So you're sayin' sex takes away our right to choose?"

"No, I'm sayin' I'm tired o' being tricked." Z-Pac steamed. "I'm tired of starting out with sex and ending up with nothing! And when I get outta here, I ain't messing with no man…not ever again…that ain't married to me!"

About this time, the scrawny dyed blonde with the six-inch lashes stepped up to Z-Pac and went nose to nose. "I'm sick o' yo mouth!" She squawked. "And if y'all follow behind this Thick-Chick, every one o' y'all gonna end up a lonely, hot-mess just like her crazy, broke-down—"

Uh-oh!

Braids and sew-ins, tattoos and nose-rings were about to throw-down when suddenly the room went silent. It was like somebody turned the volume down on the headset. The ultra-quiet one with the smooth pageboy, Keara *Kee-Kee* Brown, had been plastered against the rear wall. But she put the cap on the discussion when she finally piped up and said, "Ain't none of this ever gonna change…for us or our kids…unless men change."

Maybe Kee-Kee hadn't entered the discussion before that moment because she felt she'd heard it all before, and she didn't have a dog in the hunt; or maybe she was just laying in the cut, biding her time until she could go on her merry way. Kee-Kee was 25 years old, and this was her third time at Dipped in the Fire. She had three children by three different baby-daddies, and each one of the men had been abusive either to her or her children—and the last one, both.

After Kee-Kee had issued her startling revelation, all eyes flashed back on Wanza who was standing at the podium, slack-jawed. She couldn't have hoped for a more lively discussion to get at the problems in the current culture. The room seemed to be divided into three camps: those for kickin-it as a lifestyle—*any love is better than no love/marriage ain't nuttin' but a piece o' paper*; those who sided with Z-Pac—*kickin-it is not in the best interest of women and their kids*; and those like quiet Kee-Kee Brown—*who didn't think the culture could ever change unless men changed their attitudes toward women and children.*

"I couldn't have presented a better argument for changing your lifestyles than you've done here tonight." Wanza praised the ladies. "All I can add is that this *kickin-it* phenomenon is shaping the fabric of our lives and our communities. It's leading women and children into undefined, misguided relationships…no clear direction…no boundaries…no structure…no protection…no help. The fastest growing homeless population is women and children, which means women and their children are bearing the burden for the breakdown of the family structure. And society is getting fed-up with it…paying for it...cleaning up after it...dealing with the damaged lives it causes."

Wanza sighed aloud. "You beautiful ladies could be in college right now, or in trade school, or owning your own businesses. But you're sitting around waiting on an itty-bitty check that no one really wants to give you in the first place. And sometimes I believe that's exactly how the power brokers like it because you, smart ladies, would be a force to reckon with in the marketplace." Wanza flailed her hands in desperation. "But, now, your man is not looking out for your best interest; the state is not looking out for your best interest; and society is trying to figure out how we got here and how they can turn back the clock. And all the while, your children are suffering."

"But if you don't want this kind of life," Wanza stated blunted, "you've got to have an object in view and set some clear goals for getting there. You and your children are a family. And you're on a mission to help them grow into well-adjusted, productive members of society. And any man that steps to you, you must decide whether or not he fits into your mission."

"I can't make you do this." Wanza leveled her challenge to the group. "But if you're interested in setting a new course for your life, I want you to put a star by your name on the sign-in sheet; and we'll get started. Together, we can map out the vision and goals for you to build a better future for you and your children." *And, man-o-man, I cannot wait to tell Pastor Meadows about the breakthrough we've had here on tonight.*

CHAPTER 10
Dipped in the Fire

"Well, did you hear it, Pastor?" Wanza said as she claimed her favorite seat in front of Pastor Meadow's cluttered desk. His blue tissue box was the only item holding sentry in its proper place.

"Hear what?" Pastor Meadows said slowly. He'd learned to mind his p's and q's when dealing with Wanza Johnson-Grand because he never knew where she'd try to take him.

"We had a huge breakthrough over at Dipped in the Fire, and I was sure everyone in town must've heard the explosion." She teased.

"So…what happened," the pastor said warily.

"I wish you could've been a fly on the wall, Pastor." Wanza grinned. "We had a fiery discussion at our Orientation Meeting the other night. The young ladies were pouring out their hearts and letting the whole truth hang out."

"Sounds good."

"We got to talking about women and children being the fastest growing homeless population in America—"

"Uh-huh."

"They started to see that this whole idea of *kickin-it* has not been working in their favor—"

"And that is good news."

"We even got to talking about how the kickin-it culture is wreaking havoc on everybody." Wanza was on a roll. "How these absentee dads and toxic moms are a terrible combination that's bringing society to its knees—socially and financially. What was intended to be a stop-gap measure in case of emergency to help unwed mothers and children has become a way of life. And all this talent, and beauty, and smarts…all this potential…is just going to waste because they're not positioning themselves for greatness—"

"And that's what I've been saying." Pastor Meadows broke in. "This phenomenon is not a money issue; it goes deeper than that. This is a spiritual, moral and social issue—"

"And as our heated discussion rocked back and forth," Wanza said, reclaiming her thought, "some of the ladies were still in favor of kickin-it. But then, there was this new young lady, Z-Pac, and she and her crew were holding fast against it. In fact, Z-Pac came out and proclaimed that she's *never* going back to kickin-it when she gets back out on the streets. But—"

"But—" Pastor Meadows cut in to force her to take a breath.

"But then...this one young lady, Kee-Kee Brown, spoke up." Wanza explained. "Don't know if you recall, but this is Kee-Kee's third time with us. She's 25 and has three babies by three different baby-daddies; and, unfortunately, violence has marred every one of the relationships."

"Too bad—"

"So Kee-Kee doesn't say much, you know." Wanza recounted. "She's the type that keeps her head down and just tries to get through—"

"I understand."

"But, Pastor, if I tell you!" Wanza exclaimed. "She said a mouthful that night."

"Oh?"

"After all the other ladies had exhausted themselves, Kee-Kee spoke up and said, 'Ain't none of this gonna change unless the men change—'"

"And she oughta know."

"Right!" Wanza nodded. "And that got me to thinking. We're over here at Dipped in the Fire giving it our all, trying to get these young mothers and their children on track; only for them to go back out into the *real world* to be faced with the same culture all over again. No wonder nothing ever changes."

"So what's your point?" Pastor Meadows was beginning to feel like a hog being led to the slaughter.

"We need to go hard after the men."

"So, now, you want to go after the men?"

"No, Pastor." Wanza gave him a little wink. "I want *you* to go after the men."

"Well, I can see you're mighty gung-ho about this, but that might take some doing."

"But why?"

"Because with the men, we've got to go all the way back to the beginning…back to Genesis."

"Huh?"

"Back to when God gave men dominion over the earth." Pastor Meadows explained. "Back to when God made men the head of their families—"

"But it doesn't look like men are trying to head-up families these days—"

"No, they're acting more like bees than men—"

"Bees?"

"They just wanna hit on every pretty flower they see and keep it moving."

"But we have to change that, Pastor, if these young mothers and their children are going to find any lasting relief."

"I see your point." Pastor Meadows leaned back in his big leather chair. "But we can't inspire people into change. People can't love…men or women…if there's no love inside of them.

"But I don't understand—"

"Change, my dear Wanza, starts in the hearts and minds of people, and only Jesus can change us at the core. We may have the will or desire to change, but only Jesus can give us the power to change—"

"So you're saying we should do nothing…not even try?"

"No, I'm saying that our efforts should start with introducing people to Jesus Christ." Pastor Meadows drew out a tissue and mopped his bald head. "Your point is valid, but you can't change a man from the outside. We can make them aware...give them information on what their behavior is doing to their women...to their children...to society. We can let them know what God has to say about the matter...that sex before marriage can create all kinds of consequences—"

"Lots of consequences can happen inside a marriage, too," Wanza said, and Pastor Meadows could feel the wealth of her sadness. He knew that Douglas had hurt her deeply.

"Yes, but at least we should aim for the bullseye; even though, we all fall short, Sister Wanza."

"I guess you're right, Pastor."

"I know I'm right." Pastor Meadows gave her a smile. "Wanza, you and Y are blessed women. You've been delivered to do the good works the Lord has ordained for you. But not for you to get in a hurry...but for you to do it His way."

"I know, Pastor—"

"So you see we can't change their behavior...that's an inside job...that's the Holy Spirit's job...and you can't get the gift of the Holy Spirit until you've accepted Jesus Christ as your Saviour." Pastor Meadows exhaled. "Then, and only then, will the information we give them about changing their lifestyle and their worldview start to make any sense." Pastor Meadows chortled. "Because people can't accept God's word and His way unless they're called—"

"So why does God tell us to love everybody?"

"Because we don't know who He calls, and that's none of our business." The pastor cautioned. "Our part in it is to share the Lord's word and love in the world, because judging and hating on folk will certainly not change them."

"But—"

"But I can tell you this for a fact." Pastor Meadows pressed his point. "Men don't base their life decisions on sex. They can have their way with a woman this minute; get up; wipe their mouth; and go on about their merry way like it never happened."

"That's what I've been trying to tell the ladies!" Wanza agreed.

"But when two people come together, it's more than just sex; it's a marrying of the soul," the pastor said. "And each new partner takes a little bite out of your soul. And to fill that void, some folk drink, some party, some play...and some work real hard." He cast a suspecting eye on Wanza. "And some even use more sex...but only the Lord can restore your soul. That's why these women...and men...are so broken."

"I've got an idea!" Wanza snapped her fingers, and the preacher let out an audible groan.

"What now, Wanza?" The beleaguered preacher grimaced.

"You're right, Pastor," she said jubilantly. "We'll start off by offering the ladies a relationship with Jesus Christ. And then the training will show them how to build a better life on the basis of their faith. We'll call it...*Building Your Life Plan.*"

"O-kay—"

"I can help the young ladies build on their faith by putting together a plan and goals for themselves and their children." Wanza explained. "And you can help the men better envision their roles and responsibilities for their families with the hope that our culture can change going forward." Wanza gave her pastor and trusted friend a broad smile. "How does that sound?"

"Sounds like a lot of work." Pastor Meadows groaned. "But I can get the other pastors and ministries involved. We can break the men down by age groups—" He nodded. "And, now, that you mention it; it sounds like work that's long overdue."

"Yes!" Wanza cheered.

CHAPTER 11
The Grand Getaway

Meanwhile, Douglas Grand was enjoying Paris in the springtime. He'd arrived at the Paris Charles de Gaulle Airport in time to have a late lunch. Although his assistant, Chad, had made the arrangements, he thought Douglas' travel plans were ill-advised. They were at a tipping point in the major Smooth Jazz deal, and Chad had been prodding Douglas for weeks to make some critical decisions. But Chad knew how far to go. He knew to steer clear of Douglas' mean streak; the one that always surfaced when he couldn't get his way. But his increasing inattentiveness to details was totally unlike Douglas, and his business was starting to suffer. Chad tried to keep the deal on track, but when Douglas learned of the Paris stop on Ryhema's concert tour, all bets were off. He could think of little else. Douglas had but one thing on his mind. *Ravishing Ryhema.*

Douglas checked into the five-star Shangri-La Hotel because his sources had advised him that Ryhema had checked into a luxury suite there a few days earlier. By all accounts, it was one of her favorite spots. She adored its scenic beauty. The hotel palace was located across from the Seine River, facing the Eiffel Tower.

On his cab ride in from the airport, Douglas was impressed by the cherry blossoms in bloom along the Champ de Mars with the Eiffel Tower in the background. *How romantic!* And with the proper credentials in hand, Douglas conned and bribed his way into Ryhema's suite to set-up for the evening of lovemaking that had become his single obsession. While he waited, random thoughts toyed at the edges of his mind; thoughts of how he'd left it with his wife on the previous night.

****

"But if you're going to France, anyhow." Willamina had reasoned. "Why can't I go with you? We can have the honeymoon we'd planned for in Nice right there in Paris—"

"Ba-be." Douglas had strongly protested. "This trip is strictly business. I don't plan to be there more than one or two nights, possibly three," he said. *Or as long as it takes me to get Ryhema into my bed.* "There's just not enough time for us to squeeze in our honeymoon." He'd grazed her cheek with a gentle hand. "Don't you understand, Darling? I don't want us to be rushed."

"I understand it." Willamina's mountain twang started to resurface. "But gosh-darn-it, I don't like it. We've been married nearly six months and still no honeymoon to show for it—"

"I don't like it either, Babe." Douglas buttered his voice with the appropriate whine. "But this is business…strictly business…and I want to be over there and back so I can get home to you as quickly as possible—"

"Oh…okay." Willamina caved. "But can't I just go over and back with you?" she said hopefully. "I'd love to see Paris, too. I ain't never been to Europe, yet."

"Hmm…not this time, Babe." Douglas held up the three fingers on his right hand like a Boy Scout. "But I will not enter France again without you," he said. "I promise."

"Well…alright." Willamina smiled sweetly and opened her robe to expose her firm, glistening flesh. She hadn't slept with Douglas until their wedding night because she thought it was the right thing to do. But she had no idea there were men in the world who'd marry a woman for just one spectacular night. "Then let's just make the most of this night together." She cooed, inviting her husband to come inside.

"No…no can do, Hon." Douglas put her off casually, but firmly. He could think of nothing and no one until he'd scratched his itch for

Ryhema. "Gotta get all my ducks in a row tonight," he said, while busily clicking away on his keyboard. "Essex is whisking me off to the airport before dawn." *And that's the problem with marriage…no sooner than you land one…a better one pops up. Ha!*

****

But, now, Douglas was where he wanted to be; where he'd dreamed of being. He was squirreled away in Ryhema's elegant suite in Paris, preparing to surprise her after her last performance.

"What are you doing here?" Ryhema gasped as soon as she opened the door to her room.

"Hey, Gorgeous." Douglas' sexy voice rumbled like deep waters as he rose from the chaise lounge where he'd draped himself. He went over to a silver tray and popped the cork on a bottle of the finest Dom Pérignon. He poured the rich champagne into two crystal flutes. "I came over to see your first show." Douglas offered her a glass. "I've never seen you perform in person before." He admitted. "Long overdue. And you were brilliant! Just brilliant! You are indeed my very own shining star!"

"What are you doing…in here?" Ryhema repeated her question more directly. "In my room?"

"I paid for it; remember?" Douglas gave her a wicked smile and extended the glass.

"Where's your wife?" Ryhema stiffened.

"In Houston." Douglas checked the platinum timepiece on his left wrist. "Going on stage, right about now."

Noiselessly, Ryhema stepped forward and accepted the champagne from his waiting hand.

In a grand gesture, Douglas whisked off the linen cover from a table loaded with exquisite goodies—caviar, smoked salmon with capers, fresh pastries and other French delectables too numerous to mention.

"No, thank you," Ryhema said, turning her back on the food. She took a tiny sip of the champagne. "I rarely eat after a performance." She kicked off her Louboutin red-bottom stilettos to make a clear statement of her intentions. "I sleep."

"Re-lax." Douglas' voice rippled like waves on a secluded beach. "I want this to be a perfect evening for you…anything…anything you want." He clenched a chocolate-covered strawberry between his teeth and stepped closer to Ryhema.

For a silent heartbeat, Ryhema didn't move. She knew what would come next. But finally, she stepped toward Douglas and accepted the other half of the strawberry meant for her.

And Douglas kissed her—hard, passionately and deep. Her tussled, color-streaked hair fell in heaps around her slender, brown-sugar shoulders. When Douglas let her up for air, he reached under the silk pillow on her bed and pulled out a red, peek-a-boo negligee. He swung it on his index finger like it was a rare jewel. "I want to see you in this." His voice dipped hoarsely. "Before I rip it off you." He drew her into another steamy embrace and sucked her rosebud lips into his firm, hard ones. Her complete surrender made his body tremble. When he released her from their fiery kiss, Ryhema willingly followed his lead. She lifted the gift from his finger and gave it a slight twirl. Her lean, slinky body left behind a whiff of sweetness as she sauntered her perky butt into the powder room to change.

My-My…black & beautiful…tasty & rich…with nearly as much paper as Pretty Miss Redd…and with my backing, she could have even more influence. Oh, yes, we're gonna make this a night to remember.

****

Meanwhile, down in Houston, Texas, Willamina had tagged onto Stevie Ray Holcomb's concert tour at the White Oak Music Hall. It was just too sad and too boring for her to spend another minute in Nashville alone. The incessant days and nights of loneliness were beginning to cling to her like a tattered garment—the piercing loneliness of being married to a man who put his career above all else. Of course, she understood his business concerns; his need to raise the bar on his success, higher and higher. But she should be in France with Douglas on their long-awaited honeymoon. Instead, she was trying to make the best of a bad situation. She had Essex take her to the airport, and Stevie Ray welcomed her with open arms. They'd won a Grammy together the previous year. And when they sang their hit duet, "Where Were You When I Needed You," their country fans went totally ballistic. They brought the house down!

And after their phenomenal performance, Willamina was celebrated back in The Green Room by fans, fellow performers and musicians, alike; people she'd known in the business for years. It was like old home week, and it did her heart good to be around people who genuinely loved her, including her own family. In no time flat, she was surrounded by the same five crazy cousins that had been at her wedding reception; and as usual, Cousin Jeb did all the talking.

"Willamina, Darling, you didn't think you'd get to Houston and we wouldn't come over here to see ya; now, did ya?" Cousin Jeb said, swinging Willamina off her feet. Her red curls, which had been pinned up for the concert, were now down around her smooth, white shoulders.

"Good to see y'all, too." Willamina chirped. "I woulda been mad as a trapped skunk if y'all hadna come. That's why I left you them tickets at the Will Call." Willamina fell right into their hill-country vernacular.

"I know, Girl," Cousin Jeb said, "and we was more than happy to oblige; ain't that right, Boys?" Bubba-Dean bobbled his head, and John-Earl's glass eye twinkled under his scraggly hair when he offered his favorite cousin a jagged smile.

"So where's that husband o' your'n?" Cousin Jeb jabbed. "That ni—*nice man with the brilliant future?*" Jeb repeated, making her eat her words. "So why ain't he here with ya?"

"Oh…Douglas…he's outta the country on business." Willamina gave him the brightest smile she could muster. It was hard to lie to her family about the way she was really feeling, but Cousin Jeb couldn't be fooled.

"Look like we betta keep a tighter eye on thangs—"

"Yep, it do." Cousin John-Earl parroted, and Bubba-Dean bobbled his head. While the quiet ones, Cousin Jabbo with the long white beard hanging over his pressed overalls, and Cousin Jo-Jo, suspected by Douglas as being the inbred one, maintained their silent, yet stoic, posts.

Willamina gathered them all into one big group hug. She was so proud of her family. They reminded her that she had roots. She was grounded; and if no one else cared about her, she knew she would always hold a dear place in their hearts. And she was happy to be in this special place—around country folk—where she was loved and celebrated and not merely tolerated.

CHAPTER 12
The Mann Method

Meanwhile back in Nashville, Wanza was furious! She was so irate she didn't know where to turn. She couldn't talk to Pastor Meadows, because in the foul mood she was in her bad language would probably re-grow hair on the poor man's head. Besides, it was nearly 10 o'clock Friday night, and his sweet wife, Candi, just might not understand. Wanza reached for the phone, but she had no one to call. Finally, she scrambled into her desk drawer to find the number she'd discarded so hastily. Her hand trembled as she dialed it. It was her very last resort, and she hated having to use it; but she had no choice.

"Hullo."

"Ahh…hello…is this Money?"

"Sho' it's Money." He snapped at what he thought to be a late night sales call. "You dialed my number; didn't you?"

"Money." She hesitated. "This is me…Wanza Johnson-Grand."

"Oh." Money's spine straightened as though she could see him through the phone. "Hi there, Wanza. Good to hear from you."

"Money…I hate to bother you like this, especially at this time o' night, but I need to talk to somebody—"

"Then let it be me."

"Can you meet me in my office…over here at Dipped in the Fire…in about half an hour?"

"Sure thing." Money agreed. "I'll be there."

When Money arrived, Wanza's back was to her office door so he entered behind a quick knock and a crooked smile. "You called. I came."

"Oh, hey…come in, Money." Wanza settled in the chair behind her desk. "Sorry to get you out this late—"

"No need to explain." Money took a seat. "I was happy to hear from you."

"Well, you might not be so happy when this is over." Wanza's steam erupted. "Do you know what that Z-Pac went and did?"

"You mean that big girl with the smart mouth—"

"Yes!" Wanza screeched. "Who else?"

"Okay-Okay." Money's eyes buckled under her rage. "What did she do that's got you so smoked?"

"She was so cock-sure of herself. She had such a made up mind. 'I'm Z-Pac.' She boasted. 'I can stand my ground, Ms. Wanza.' She said." Wanza recounted her many affirmations. "And at every session, Z-Pac was stone-cold serious about building her life plan." Wanza hopped up from her chair. "And now…now…she went and got herself pregnant; that's what she did!" Wanza screamed. "I had such high hopes for that girl. And after all her big talk—" Wanza parroted the young woman's brazen tone. "'I ain't letting no man touch me no mo! When I get outta here, no mo kickin-it for me!' And Z-Pac even got some of the other ladies buying into her big talk! And, now, what're they gonna think?" Wanza raged. "And after all that, the girl goes out, and the first thing she does is get herself knocked-up by some guy she don't even know!"

"Huh?"

"And then she calls me…crying! And I asked her, Z-Pac, what's his name, Girl?" Wanza was flailing her hands and flashing her eyes. Her 'hood was now in full effect. "And she say, 'I dunno…they call him *Juice*.' And I say, where he live Z-Pac? And she say, 'I dunno; I met him at the pool hall.' Do you hear that, Money? She's pregnant by some fly-by-night joker from the dad-gum pool hall! She ain't the main-chick! She ain't the side-chick! She ain't no chick 'cause she don't even know the boy's last name!" Wanza wailed. "Have you ever heard of anything so whack in your en-tire life?" She screamed. "Well, have you?"

"Wanza." Money dared answer. "Sometimes…we think we're in control…but we're really in trouble…and we just don't know it—"

"And sometimes we're just stupid!" Wanza retorted. "Six months of her hard work…and my precious time…just to see it all go up in smoke!"

"Sometimes…people stay in their mess 'cause they feel like they've gone too far." Money reflected on his own years of rebellion. "They don't know how to turn around…they don't know how to get back. And they don't know that they can accept Jesus and start their life all over again—"

"W-h-a-t?"

"And they're too afraid…or too stubborn…to accept His free gift." Money's voice hollowed. "Because they feel like it's something they've gotta do, and they fear they're just not good enough to do it. So instead of getting out, they get in deeper…'cause they feel like there ain't no hope—"

"That's a real pretty speech, Money." Wanza fumed. "But what's that gotta do with Z-Pac, now? The girl's already got herself pregnant!"

"I ain't gonna try to tell you to calm down, Wanza, 'cause I can see you're all up in yo feelings," Money said evenly. "And I feel for you, too…I really do. But, Wanza, you know there ain't nuttin' you can do 'bout it; now, don't you?"

"But it's just such a waste—"

"And you're mad—"

"I am not mad!" Wanza shouted.

"Ok, then." Money smiled on the inside at the lady's tenacity and perseverance. "So you're sad…disappointed 'cause you couldn't hold it together for Z-Pac—"

"Maybe—"

"But we can't hold it together for other folk, Wanza." Money chomped down on his toothpick. "Shucks…we can't even hold it together for ourselves." He recalled his own past failures. "Holding it together…that just ain't our job—"

"So what're we supposed to do?" Wanza fumed. "Throw up our hands and give up?"

"Naw." Money began and with every passing word he could feel the tide turning in his own heart. "We've just gotta trust the Lord…accept what we've been given…and thank Him for whatever He gives…or whatever He takes away." *Even if it's my po' Missy.*

"Of course, you're right, Money." Wanza relented, feeling convicted for indulging in her rage and in her momentary lapse of faith. "The Lord has *all* power and by Him *all* things consist." She recounted one of Pastor Meadow's sermon topics.

"So only the Lord has the power to hold things together, huh?"

"Oh, I know." Wanza dropped back into her chair. The calm in Money's voice brought her where she needed to be. She was happy to talk to a man who understood. A man she didn't have to explain herself to or censor her words. A man who was trying to build her up and not tear her down…*like D-O-U-G.* "But I try so hard with these girls, Money." Her disappointment was finally breaking down into tears. "I try so hard to help them get their lives back on track—"

"I know you do, Wanza," Money said quietly. "But I know you realize that's not all there is to it; now, don't you?"

"Whatcha mean?"

"You can plant good seeds—"

"But I can't make 'em grow." Wanza finished the biblical treatise; another one she'd learned from Pastor Meadows. "Only God gives the increase."

"Sometimes…people have to go through things…hard things." Money continued out of the wealth of his experience. "'Cause only the Lord knows how we learn. And He keeps on stripping away and stripping away at all our foolishness…until we finally get it—"

"Until we finally yield." Wanza settled.

"Until we learn to do things His way—"

"I've been trying to pull the string straight and tight for these ladies." Wanza conceded. "But you're right, Money. The string ain't even in my hands—"

"It's in God's hands—"

"Yep."

"I didn't begin to live…until I was willing to give up on my old life." Money admitted grudgingly.

"What life?"

"Ahh…I think you know." Money twirled his toothpick. "But I've served my time. I'm not a danger to society anymore. I'm working. I'm volunteering. I'm trying to make amends for some o' my wrongdoing. I'll never balance the scales, but I'm trying. But I had to get to this place on my own…with the help of the Lord. Maybe, your Z-Pac just ain't got there yet.

"What did you do…to go to prison, I mean?"

"Nothing really violent." Money explained. "Just fell in with a bad crowd the first time. And then there was that period where I used to booze it up and got popped for having a li'l pharma stash on the side, ya know…for my own personal use—"

"And all that's behind you?"

"Yes, ma'am. No mo demon rum for me, and no mo three strikes and you're out. That life behind bars…any kind o' bars…is not for me. Besides, I owe it to—" Money bit his tongue; it was too soon to let Missy's name slip. "I owe it to myself to start living a life I can be proud of."

"And nobody pulled your string straight?" Wanza glimmered.

"Well, there's these two ladies in my hometown—the Whatnot sisters—they helped me see that the prison tats may remain, but I'm not a prisoner to my past…not anymore. And I can trust Jesus to lead me into a bright, new future. That's what your ladies have gotta accept, too."

"Where did you grow up?" Wanza was warming up to Money's quiet resolve.

"Knoxville. Preacher's kid—"

"You?"

"Yup...but it's a long story."

"I guess we've both been suffering under some misconceptions." Wanza squeaked. "I didn't know you were a preacher's kid...and you think I'm this fine lady who's always been on top." She chuckled. "But I may not be who you think I am—"

"How's that?"

"I haven't always been what you see here today: the woman with the college degree; the woman with the big mansion on Legends Way; the woman who directs a women's ministry. The Lord has had to bring me from a l-o-n-g way off. I didn't even get saved 'til I came to True Vine...following behind D-o-u-g and that hussy, Melissa—"

"Oh?" Money nearly swallowed his toothpick. It stung like a bullet hearing his sister's name mentioned in that context, but he managed to keep his cool.

"Yeah...and I've had to learn a lot of lessons from the school of hard knocks." Wanza breathed out her closely-held disclosure. "Bet you didn't know I grew up in the North Nashville projects with seven siblings, an absent daddy and a cracked-out mamma—"

"I know." Money eyed her closely. Some wild wigs and about 50 pounds were missing, but he wasn't ready to tell Wanza that he'd spied on her at Missy's request and had also checked into her background. He didn't want to take any chance of losing her before they even got started.

"What? How do you know?"

"I've been watching ya." Money clicked his toothpick. "Up close and personal. And can't no woman throw-down on these young women and keep 'em in line like I see you do unless she's got a li'l 'hood in her somewhere—"

"Sho' you right." Wanza snapped her neck and gave him a sassy wink.

"But it still would be wrong of me to think I could have a chance with a fine lady like you." Money laid his soulful eyes into his lap.

"Why do you say a thing like that?" Wanza gave him a glimmer of hope. "You're the one who grew up on the right side of the tracks...the preacher's kid—"

"Yeah, but there's more to it than you know—"

"That may be so, but you were born with the silver spoon in your mouth. You were the one in the family with the requisite 2.0 kids. You were the one who knew which fork to use at dinner—"

"Yeah, but in that prison mess, my only concern was that nobody stuck that fork in my back."

"But that's my point," Money." Wanza insisted. "I've come a long way up from my beginnings, and you've come a long way back to get to this point; so that makes us even. So quit thinking I'm too good for you...or that anybody is too good for us. We both love the Lord and that makes us equal."

Money eased his tattooed hands onto Wanza's desk. "If you really believe that," he said, "give me yo hands."

Wanza was hesitant because she recalled how his touch had made her feel when he'd handed her his phone number. "Alright." She eased both hands onto the desk in his direction, and Money did the rest.

"You are one mo pretty lady, Miss Wanza." He linked his fingers into hers. "And I do think you're right. You can't hold a man back from a woman he really wants to be with."

"Quit that, Money." Wanza giggled, but she didn't move her hands.

CHAPTER 13
The Grand Hideaway

Summer was budding in Nashville, and the scent of lovemaking was in the air. Essex could only glimpse the movement of the shadowy figures through the tinted partition of the Rolls Royce he was chauffeuring, but their groans and moans gave him a hint as to what was going on. At Mizter G's instruction, Essex had driven him to the Nashville International Airport to pick up Ryhema on her return trip from Madrid, Spain. From the moment they laid eyes on each other, Essex could see that they were lovers. *No one fools a boy from NOLA...pas un imbécile.* But he catered to their needs like they were any other passengers in the vehicle he was driving.

When they got to the Hotel Carlisle, one of Douglas' favorite locations for business—and other endeavors—Essex opened the rear door widely for Ryhema and Douglas to exit. He carried no expression on his face other than that of a faithful bodyguard-chauffeur. "May I help you with your things?" Essex offered when Douglas exited the vehicle.

"No, not tonight," Douglas said, sniffing the warm night air like a man on top of the world. "We'll let the hotel valet handle the ladies things."

A dog is known to return to his old haunts, but Douglas could ill afford for his love nest to be found out. When he was married to Wanza on Legends Way, his hideaway at the Hotel Carlisle was nearly an hour's drive away. But its proximity to his current residence at Opryland Towers made it almost too close for comfort. So Douglas took some added precautions not to be discovered. Routinely, he'd use the back entrance to the hotel and the pass key to the rear service elevator, which he'd bribed from a service attendant on a previous occasion. And after following his surreptitious route, he'd slide into his assigned suite with Ryhema—Room 306.

"Very well, Mizter G." Essex answered tightly.

"And Essex, my man." Douglas buzzed in his ear. "What goes on in the backseat of my car is my business. Is that clear?"

"Yes, Boss."

"That means you don't tell anybody...including my darling wife. Got that straight?" Douglas said, slowly and firmly. He'd always sensed Essex's intense loyalty and blind attraction to Willamina from the start of their arrangement, and he could not afford for it to interfere with his secret affair with Ryhema.

"I got it, Mizter G." Essex resented being treated like a third grader.

"And just so you don't think you've got anything hanging over my head—" Douglas stopped suddenly and looked around. The short hairs on the back of his neck were prickling, and he had the strange sensation that he was being watched. But he shrugged it off. He knew Willamina was totally in the dark about his clandestine routines; and besides, he knew she had too much class to have him followed. "But like I said, Essex," Douglas repeated, "you've got nothing on me."

"Why do you say these things to me, Boss?" Essex said, eyeing his strange behavior.

"Me and Willamina have things worked out; that's why." Douglas boasted. "We have an open-marriage, but I don't rub her nose in it." He shrugged. "We're on the road a lot. She does her thing, and I do mine." Douglas gritted his teeth. "So if you're thinking of telling her anything, it won't make a bit of difference. Is that clear?"

"No worries, Boss," was Essex's singular reply as he scanned the sidewalk for the prying eyes he felt on him. He'd been having that eerie feeling a lot of late; and he didn't like it, not one little bit. He hoped it wasn't that Money-creature coming back for another taste of Mizter G. But whoever it was, he was ready. He felt along the edges of his shoulder holster and patted his trusty pistol.

Douglas smiled from within as he joined the waiting Ryhema on the curb. *I wonder how long it will take this New Orleans lady's man to go after Pretty Miss Redd, now? A few more lonely nights...and I've got her prime to accept...and when she falls for his charms, the prenup will kick-in. I'll walk away a free man...with half her worldly goods...including those 21% voting shares that are rightfully mine. It's about time I got those li'l babies in my hands where they belong...them and my Ravishing Ryhema.*

CHAPTER 14
The Grand Opening

Willamina had to make a quick trip over to True Vine to meet with Pastor Meadows, but she was bushed. All the travel, all the performances—all the uncertainty in her marriage—was taking its toll. She was headed for her Bentley when she saw Essex driving the Rolls onto the driveway at Opryland Towers. He had just returned from dropping Douglas off at the Nashville International Airport, bound for Munich, Germany. Unbeknownst to Willamina, Ryhema was performing there.

"Good afternoon, Miz G." Essex called.

"Afternoon, Essex." Willamina returned with a wave.

"Where are you headed?" Essex inquired. "May I be of service?"

"Oh, Essex." Willamina wavered. "Would you? I hate to ask you…just to drive me over to True Vine…but I'm tired as an old cat." She explained. "I've just got to talk to Pastor Meadows about volunteering at Dipped in the Fire now that my calendar is clearing up a might. I won't be long."

"It would be my pleasure to drive you, Miz G, and you take all of the time that you need." He smiled the handsome smile that put his cleft chin on full display. His ebony, chiseled skin glistened in the bright sunlight. "I am sure to enjoy the beauty of Brentwood. C'est belle!"

"Well, it's settled then." Willamina bounced into the front passenger seat of her Bentley and tossed Essex the keys." She had on a flouncy red skimmer with red eel-skinned ankle boots and smooth, bare legs, which did not escape Essex's notice.

"Do you not want to ride in the rear?" Essex reminded her when he felt his heart flutter with excitement. "It would be most proper, you know."

"We don't have to be so formal; do we, Essex?" Willamina groaned. "What's a short ride between friends?"

"Suit yourself, Madame." He teased and vowed to himself to keep his eyes front and center, like a good soldier. Given what her husband was up to with Ryhema, he didn't want to disrespect the lady also.

While he waited for Willamina to return from her meeting with Pastor Meadows, Essex kicked the tires on her Bentley and recalled his interesting lunch earlier in the day. After he'd dropped off Mizter G at the airport, he'd swung by his favorite fusion Chinese joint on Church Street. The establishment was owned by a Creole brother and his Chinese wife, and Essex had indulged in his menu favorite—*Soul Fried Rice*—chock full of juicy shrimp and Creole seasonings. But more importantly, his fortune cookie had read, "This is your lucky day. Take a chance!" And seeing as how his beloved Grand Ma-Ma had taught him never to tempt fate, Essex was beginning to believe that this was the day he should bare his heart and soul to Miz G. He would never want to upset her, but he needed to make his intentions known. *I must offer her the love in my heart...tout de suite...even if I have only a sliver of a chance.*

When Willamina returned to the car, she resumed the passenger seat, and Essex opened the sunroof to let the warm Nashville breezes flow through. The perennial showers of spring had given way to the richness of the summer skies. He tightened his hands on the wheel, trying not to give his passenger any notice. "I know Mizter G has lots of other interests and is out of town a lot." Essex swallowed hard and squeezed out the words. "I just want you to know...that I am here for you, Miz G...if you should ever need...if you should ever need my company—"

"Wait one minute!" Willamina set straight up in the passenger seat; her blue eyes wide and fearful. "Essex...I fancied us to be friends. What are you tryna say here?"

"I think you're the prettiest woman I've ever seen in my whole life." Essex poured out his heart that was thudding against his massive chest. "You must know how I have felt about you...even from the first...from that very first day I laid my eyes upon you—"

"But you know I'm a married woman—"

"And your husband, he is a married man...but what has that got to do with anything?"

"It has everything to do with it!" Willamina bristled. "I'm surprised at you Essex—"

"But—"

"But what?" Willamina self-consciously tugged on her short skirt. "Just drive me home. What must you be thinking?"

"But he told me—" Essex said before he could stop himself. "He told me that you have a marriage...a marriage which does not have walls."

Willamina knew deep in her heart that she had nothing to fear from Essex, not really; so she put her back to the passenger door and looked at him straight on. "Are you telling me that Douglas Grand told you that we have...an open marriage?"

"Yes...that is it...an open marriage." Essex squeezed the steering wheel in his massive hands. "He did say it...but it was wrong...wrong of me to break his confidence—"

"His confidence?!?" The screech in Willamina's drawl reached as high as the Tennessee mountains. "What about my confidence?!? What about the vow that low-down, snake-in-the-grass made to me—"

"I am so sorry." Essex apologized profusely. "Mizter G warned me not to speak of it...it was not my place—"

"No, Essex." Willamina softened her tone, trying to ease the man's mind. "Did Douglas tell you to make a play for me like this?"

90

"Oh, no!" A smile creased at the edges of Essex's strong mouth, and he finally turned to meet Willamina's troubled blue eyes head on. "That idea, Miz G, was all mine…mine alone."

"Oh, Essex." Willamina turned her face to the window and nearly cried. "I'm afraid Douglas told you that with the hopes that you *would* make a play for me." *And I'd accept.* Her mind thrashed around for a motive for his madness. *That blasted prenup! That's it! That's why he's been tryna make me feel so lonely! He wants to make me cheat! And if I do, Douglas can get his grubby li'l hands on half o' all my worldly goods…and I can just bet which half. The coward! He wants them 21% voting shares…the ones that're still in my name!*

"I swear to you," Essex said, still endeavoring to protect his boss. "Non! Mizter G, he did not tell me to make a play for you, as you say—"

"But he knew you might…and he's been keeping me love-starved enough to make me wanna accept—"

"I am way out of line, and I am so sorry." Essex tightened his tone. "I have the highest regard for you, Miz G. I really do. You are a splendid lady—"

"And I think you're tops, too, Essex." Willamina sought to allay the man's fears. "But I'm a Christian woman, and we don't *do* open marriages. We get married…'til death do us part."

"So why…why did you marry such a man…as Mizter G?" Essex blurted, unable to forget all of the times he'd witnessed Douglas and Ryhema thrashing around in the backseat of the Rolls. "Was it his money? Was it his fame?"

"Oh, I don't know." Willamina's voice dipped like the tail on a broken balloon. "I know what it's like to come a long way from nothing, and I thought that bonded me and Douglas to walk this journey of life together. I had money. He had money. It didn't seem to make no difference. And since we went to the same church and shared the same faith…or at least I thought we did…I thought our races didn't make no difference, neither."

Willamina smiled at her sweet reminisces of her whirlwind courtship with Douglas. "I guess he just kind o' sweet talked me into believing that our marriage was a natural," she said in a hurt whisper. "I mean, since I already knew his ex-wives, and he promised me that he'd learned his lesson. He promised me he loved me more than anyone he'd ever known." She blew out a heavy sigh. "He convinced me we'd be able to stay right here together…faithful and true…right here in my beloved Nashville. And besides, we both understand the ups and downs and hardships of this business…and we'd be able to comfort each other and help each other through it…and maybe even help some other kids make it big along the way—"

"Yes, I see." Essex banged his knuckles against the steering wheel, reminding himself to pay closer attention to the rush hour traffic. He was so ashamed, and he was all out of words. But in the space of time it took to say a prayer, he said, "So what do you want me to do, now, Miz G? I sincerely apologize to you for being so way out of line. Do you want me to apologize to Mizter G? Do you want me to resign my post and never be seen or heard of again—"

"Stop it, Essex!" Willamina groaned. "You didn't do nothing wrong. There's nothing for you to apologize to me for…and certainly not to Douglas—"

"So do you want me to resign my post?"

"No! Never!" Willamina shrieked. "I want everything to stay just the way it is. I don't want Douglas to ever be the wiser that we had ourselves this li'l talk. If anything needs doing, I'll do it. Is that clear?"

"Yes, ma'am," Essex said humbly.

And with that, Willamina reached across the console and kissed Essex on his dark, burning cheek. "You're a real cool cat, Essex

LaBrie," she said. "And somewhere out there, there's a lucky woman waiting just for you. So we're gon' forget this ever happened, and we're gon' keep on with our gitty-up. Is that clear?"

"Yes, ma'am, Miz G," Essex said solemnly. "It is a privilege and honor to serve such a great lady as yourself."

"But as for Douglas, I've got his number." Willamina tossed back her shiny red curls and mumbled to herself without shedding one tear. Her husband had laid her out on the platter of Essex's raw desire like a slab of red meat. She hated to admit it to herself, but little by little, day by day, Douglas had been pushing her into the background and laying her to the side. Her kindness didn't matter. Her loyalty and understanding didn't matter. Her beauty, which Douglas had once prized, didn't matter. *I can't love this man into loving me.*

But unlike her predecessors—Wanza and Melissa—Wives #1 & #2—she was not about to get emotional and roll over and play dead. She wasn't about to allow herself to feel like damaged goods. *Oh, no; I'm a mountain woman.* And she owed it to her po-white-trash ancestors to show Douglas Grand the kind of payback that traced through her hillbilly blood. She might not possess a cast-iron skillet, like the one her Grandma Betsy had used to brain her dearly-departed husband, but she had her ways. *It's high-time I contacted my lawyer, my broker...and my pastor.*

CHAPTER 15
Double-Dipped in the Fire

It was a hot day in July when Wanza tapped on Pastor Meadows' office door. "Pastor," she said, plopping down heavily in his desk chair. "I've got some bad news to report."

"What's that Sister Wanza?" The pastor scrambled to straighten his desk so he could see her over his piles of clutter.

"I hate to bring bad tidings." Wanza continued. "But I'm afraid Z-Pac...has really messed up."

"Z-Pac?" The pastor's bushy brows knitted together. "Is she the young woman you were so proud of; the one who swore off her lifestyle of kickin-it?"

"One in the same." Wanza huffed out a big sigh. "Well...she's pregnant...again!"

"That's unfortunate," Pastor Meadows said.

"And she wants to rejoin us once she's had the baby."

"But somewhat predictable."

"Predictable?" Wanza quizzed. "Why so?"

"She was your shining flower, Wanza, because she said all the right things and made all the right moves when there was no one there to challenge her resolve."

"Shining flower, huh?"

"Yep. She made you feel good...like your brainchild...the *Building Your Life Plan* program was really starting to work—"

"But she didn't just fool me." Wanza protested. "She pulled a lot of the young ladies in on her side. They were all gonna give up kickin-it when they got back on the streets. And now that Z-Pac's gone and done this, the ladies in her camp are starting to doubt themselves—"

"And maybe that's a good thing, Wanza."

"How can that possibly be a good thing?" Wanza groaned.

"Your shining flower didn't have any roots."

"Roots?"

"You say she never accepted Jesus; right?"

"Right." Wanza shrugged. "She simply refused."

"Without accepting the Lord's love and His help, none of us has the power to break the cycle of our old ways." Pastor Meadows passed Wanza a tissue from his blue box so she could catch her budding tears. "And that's probably something the other ladies in Z-Pac's camp need to see firsthand. Sex is no game; it's not a toy. It can have some real serious consequences. And the other ladies need to see they can't make these radical lifestyle changes without the power of Jesus on their side."

"Well, I've learned my lesson, Pastor." Wanza dabbed her eyes. "I can't hold nothing together; I can't make nothing be!" She blew out a sigh that seemed to release her from the weight of the world. "All I can do is enjoy the assignment the Lord has given me…teach my classes and share His good word whenever and wherever I can. But it's not my job to predict who it's gonna fall on or who it's gonna help. And if I try to predict it, I'll be the one most miserable."

"I'd say that about sums it up, Sister Wanza." The pastor nodded his bald dome. "God didn't send us here to save the world or fix His people. We can only share His love and the gifts we've been given to share—"

"And if they need fixin'—"

"Let Jesus do it—"

"But you know what, Pastor?" Wanza tossed in. "Kee-Kee Brown did get saved."

"Now, we're talking," Pastor Meadows said jubilantly. "Is that the one that's got us trying to get the men to change their *evil* ways."

"Yup, she's the one." Wanza smiled. "And how is that going, Pastor…with the men, I mean?"

"It's taking some careful teaching." Pastor Meadows admitted. "But our *Men's Restoration Program,* which is reaching out to men in our church and the community, is starting to help the men to see the awesome role that God has given them in the world."

"And that's making a difference?"

"It surely is. The men are starting to realize they're not bees, but God has made us protectors of families and keepers of homes." Pastor Meadows sighed. "And as we talk through things, it's easy to see that the world has gotten men feeling so beat down...feeling like they're nothing and have nothing to offer. Got them thinking that they bring no value to the table when they're dealing with women...so it's bip-bam-thank-you-ma'am...'cause what else do they have to offer? And with that kind of thinking, it's no wonder they've abandoned their role as head of the household."

"But they're starting to see the light?"

"You better believe it!" Pastor Meadows whooped. "And they're starting to see that marriage is a better alternative for themselves, their women and their children...better than just kickin-it. They're starting to realize that God has a higher calling on their lives."

"Wow!" Wanza shared his enthusiasm. "At least there's some good news."

"Of course, there's good news. There's always good news! Didn't you tell me Kee-Kee got saved?"

"She did," Wanza said seriously. "It was totally unexpected, too. I told you how she's quiet and shies away from sharing her feelings—"

"Uh-huh." The pastor smiled. "But the Lord's at work while we're asleep—"

"Well, that's what happened the night Minister Yvette Soams came over to do a mandatory Bible Study." Wanza explained. "Yvette didn't make up any words of her own...none...she just read to the ladies straight outta the Bible. One by one, she read all of the scriptures that speak to who Jesus is and how much He loves us—"

"And that did it?"

"I tell you, Pastor, there wasn't a dry eye in the room by the time Yvette finished reading." Wanza recounted. "And when the invitation was extended to accept Jesus Christ as your Saviour, Kee-Kee jumped right up and ran up front to stand with Yvette. All the other ladies were so surprised…but we were all very happy, too."

"And then what happened?"

"Well, right then and there, Kee-Kee asked Yvette could she be baptized. She said she'd heard preachers before, but she'd never heard of the love and forgiveness that Jesus had for her until that night. She said, 'I wondered why my life had gotten all messy. But I've been looking for love on my own terms while the love of Jesus was right there for me all the time.'"

"Oh, really?"

"And then Kee-Kee said she didn't wanna wait to go to church. She wanted to get baptized at Dipped in the Fire where she'd crossed over from death to life…in more ways than one. Kee-Kee said she wanted the whole world to know that if nobody else loves her…Jesus loves her and her kids…and that's enough for her!"

"And what did Minister Yvette do?"

"She answered the call, of course!" Wanza exclaimed. "All of us…every one of the ladies in the room…we all got up and walked down to the kiddie pool with Kee-Kee and Minister Yvette." Wanza teared. "And in the most solemn and stirring way imaginable, Yvette baptized Kee-Kee…and we were all eyewitnesses. I tell you; it was one the most moving times I've ever experienced at Dipped in the Fire."

"So you see?"

"See what?"

"Your shining flower, Z-Pac, failed…without Jesus. But the one you would've never expected was called by our Saviour's love. God's word never returns void, but sometimes it misses the one we're aiming at and hits another. Just goes to show, we can sow the good seeds—"

"But only God gives the increase." Wanza intoned. "I think I've heard this before, Pastor, and I'm finally taking it all in."

"And what of Kee-Kee, now?"

"Well, ever since that night, she's worked really hard on her life plan. She's doing much better in court reporting school. Mrs. Lawson over at the Center is very proud of her. And she leaves us in two weeks to move into her own apartment with her three children. An apartment, I might add, she'll be able to afford out of her own paycheck!"

"That's great." Pastor Meadows laid his eyes on her. "And what about you?"

"Me?"

"How's your life progressing, Sister Wanza. You can't live through the ups-and-downs of these young ladies, you know."

"I know, Pastor." Wanza's pretty brown cheeks flushed. "I'm doing alright…and actually…I've been seeing this one man…that I'm growing quite fond of."

"Is that right?" Pastor Meadows' eyes widened. "Do I need to meet him?"

"Not just yet, Pastor." Wanza smiled. "But I'll bring him around soon. I think he'd be a great asset to your Men's Restoration Program. He's had a hard-knock life, but he's a witness to what the Lord can do…if we let him."

"Well, that's good news, indeed, Sister Wanza. Because we're all either moving toward the light and truth, or we're headed away toward darkness and death." Pastor Meadows rose to escort her to the door. "And I'm glad you stopped by today. It gets hard sitting in my seat sometimes. And I really needed to hear some good testimonies for a change."

"Thanks, Pastor." Wanza approached his door with lighter steps. "Always a pleasure.

"Oh, by the way, Wanza." Pastor Meadows stopped her at the door. "Willamina came by earlier today—"

"Willamina Redd-Grand?" Wanza tooted her lips at the thought. *D-o-u-g's third wife?*

"Yes, Wanza." The pastor gave her a cautionary look. "Where's your Christian charity?"

"Alright." Wanza rocked on one hip. "What did she want?"

"She says she's going through some things right now—"

"It's no wonder; married to the likes of D-o-u-g—"

"And she wants to slow down her schedule while she works through them—"

"Uh-huh—"

"And I applaud her for that—"

"And—"

"And…she'd like to volunteer at Dipped in the Fire." Pastor Meadows firmed. "You know she *is* one of our biggest donors—"

"I know, Pastor." Wanza let out a sly chuckle. "And I ain't got nothing at all against the woman. It's totally her problem for falling for the likes of Douglas Grand. Besides, me and Willamina were rocking along fine 'til that man showed up. So, of course, she can stop by and see me anytime. That is…if she's woman enough for the task."

"I'm quite sure she is." Pastor Meadows returned her sly glance. "I just hope you're woman enough to receive her."

"Sho' you right." Wanza winked, and the pastor shook his weary head as he showed her out of his office.

CHAPTER 16

The Mann Exposure

When Willamina Redd-Grand rolled into the reception area at Dipped in the Fire Ministries, Y's eyes flashed wide open. Of course, Wanza had told her she was expecting an important visitor, but she'd never imagined it would be Willamina. *And, oh, how beautiful she is!* It was a fair summer's day, and Willamina's gorgeous red hair was swinging over a denim empire dress that tickled her knees, and she was wearing the sharpest pair of three-quarter, eel-skinned boots Y had ever seen.

Of course, Willamina remembered Y. They had joined True Vine on the same Sunday, but in deference to her firm allegiance to Wanza, Willamina was cordial and polite, but somewhat distant. "Hello, Y," she said pleasantly. "Remember me?"

"Of course, I do, Willamina," Y said with a broad smile, but she didn't round the counter to give her a hug. "How've you been?"

"Busy as a long-tailed cat in a room full o' rockin' chairs," Willamina said to keep it light. "Guess you've been pretty busy, too; what with your two kids, and this job and all."

"Betta believe it." Y whistled. "My two keep me pretty busy, so it's a good thing I love my job."

"Glad to hear it." Willamina looked around the room. "This place is really shaping up to be a class act." She smiled. "Wanza here?"

"Oh, yes." Y morphed into her professional persona. "She's expecting you." She thumbed her toward Wanza's glass office door near the staircase.

"Thanks." Willamina waved as she followed her instructions and tapped lightly on Wanza's office door.

"Well, looky here!" Wanza stood, trying not to appear as though she'd been waiting. Wanza was sporting a lovely red dress with a wide patent belt and black and red sling-backs, which highlighted her pretty, smooth legs. She'd also made sure that the fresh cut on her shiny black 'fro was on point. She swung from behind her desk and met Willamina at the door. "Come in. Come in," she said brightly.

"How are you Wanza?" Willamina received her cordiality like a cat on tip-toes. "You're looking wonderful—"

"And you, too," Wanza said.

"And Y's looking mighty good out there behind that reception desk." Willamina continued. "In fact, everything looks mighty good around here…just great!"

"Thanks; we're giving it our all." Wanza offered her the chair facing her desk, which placed Willamina's back to her glass office door. "Have a seat."

"Well—" Willamina said warily, since this was their first face-to-face since her marriage to Douglas.

"Well—" Wanza repeated with a half-smile, sensing her old friend's uneasiness and remembering her solemn promise to Pastor Meadows to be good.

"So…how've you been—"

"Come here, Gurrl." Wanza stood up again and rounded her desk to give Willamina a big, genuine hug. "I sure have missed you."

"Whoo!" Willamina relaxed visibly and returned her warm embrace. "I've been wanting to stop by and see you, so many times, but I just didn't know—"

"Now, we're not gonna let D-o-u-g come between us; are we?"

"Well, I certainly hope not." Willamina smiled. "'Cause you're doing some great work here, and I wanna keep supporting you…and volunteer every chance I get."

"But you could tell your husband he oughta make time to come see his two boys—"

"Uh-uh, Mrs. Wanza Johnson-Grand," Willamina said, making the sign of zipping her lips. "That's how I keep my hands clean…staying outta y'all's family affairs."

"And you're a very wise woman, Mrs. Willamina Redd-Grand," Wanza returned her grin. "That was so unfair of me. I'll get my lawyer to call his lawyer—"

"There you go—"

"And I won't ever bring him up again, if you don't." Wanza squeezed her lips shut.

"Sounds like a winner to me, Gurlie." Willamina smiled, happy to have the chance to call her friend by her pet name again. "'Cause since I'm between gigs…and such…I have some time to volunteer a couple o' days a week." Willamina kept good eye contact with Wanza and a stiff upper lip; she wasn't about to let her know the inner turmoil she was battling. She hadn't even told Pastor Meadows the whole truth; that her absent husband was why she had so much time on her hands. She wanted to stay close to home and make herself available in case Douglas wanted to work things out. She knew he was up to something, but she knew it would do her no good to accuse or confront him. He was way too slippery for that. But she was determined not to take the low road of spying and digging for dirt. Instead, she'd take the high road by being of service to other hurting women, while she trusted the Lord to keep His Word to her. *"There is nothing covered that shall not be revealed; and hid that shall not be known."*

"So you wanna volunteer, heh?" Wanza nodded approvingly. "Good…'cause we sho' need your time…just like we need yo money…badder than a hog needs slop." Wanza flung one of her old sayings back at her, and they shared a big belly laugh together.

"There you go, Gurlie." Willamina giggled. "You're getting the hang of it. You're starting to sound more and more like my Cousin Jeb."

"But for real, Willamina," Wanza said, "we really do need some extra help around here because we're launching this new training—"

"Oh?"

"Yep." Wanza smiled. "We're calling it *Building Your Life Plan.* We're trying to teach our young ladies that they and their children constitute a family, and they need to set a life plan and goals for their family...and, of course, it needs to include Jesus Christ at its center."

"Of course—"

"And they should look for husbands who have a life plan, too; one that includes them and their children. 'Cause this whole idea of *kickin-it* has really turned out to be a disaster for so many women and children of this generation—"

"Sounds promising." Willamina nodded, although her stomach was pitching a hissy fit at the irony of the situation. "Every husband should certainly have a life plan and goals for his family." *But unfortunately, not every husband's plan includes being true to his wife.*

Since Wanza's desk faced the reception area, she could see Money through her glass office door when he entered. He waved, and she gave a little wave back. Instinctively, Willamina turned her head to see—

"Oh, no!" Willamina sucked in her breath like a tsunami. "Do you know that man?"

"Sure." Wanza frowned at her curious behavior. "That's Money. He volunteers as a van driver for the Women's Services Center—"

"Do you know who he is?"

"Sure. I just told you—"

"That's Money—"

"I know—"

"Money Mann." Willamina swung her head forward so he couldn't get a good look at her. "That's Melissa's brother."

"Melissa who?" Wanza said, holding out hope for a mistaken identity.

"Melissa Mann-Grand; who else?" Willamina sniped.

"It can't be." Wanza gasped, holding her head down so Money couldn't see her reactions.

"But it is—"

"But how do you know?"

"Well…Money jumped Douglas in the parking lot on our wedding day…with a gun—"

"A gun!" Wanza nearly screamed; but instead, she buried her face in the papers on her desk.

"Yes!" Willamina whispered. "But nothing really came of it. They just had a big blow-up is all." Willamina bit her lip. "And Douglas…in an attempt to lay his fears off on me and make me think he was concerned about my welfare…had his security guy print me a picture of Money. And that's him…standing out there in your reception area." She chanced another quick peek. "He's certainly cleaned-up his act from that old mug shot I saw, but that's him, alright. That's Money Mann."

"Well—" Wanza fell back so far in her chair she almost bounced off the wall.

"Don't worry, none," Willamina whispered. "Just keep calm. I don't want him to see me, neither. And I'll stay right here with ya…'til that man is long gone."

CHAPTER 17
The Mann Confession

Money wondered why Wanza had declined his dinner invitation since they'd been seeing each other nearly every night. Instead, she'd insisted that he meet her in her office after hours; and he'd accepted. The reception area was already dark when he got there, and the residents and inductees were on the upper floors or in the other wing. The lights were on in Wanza's glass-front office, but Money approached her door cautiously and gave it a slight tap-tap so as not to alarm her. "Hey, there," he said and walked in.

Before he could take his seat in front of her cluttered desk, Wanza jumped up from behind it. "Money Mann!" She screeched. "I'm gonna tear you a new one!"

"Wh-at?" Money stammered. He was shocked to hear his last name blasting from her lips, but the fire blazing in her eyes told him the rest of the story.

"Why didn't you have the decency to tell me you're Melissa Mann-Grand's brother?" Wanza yelled.

"B-ut...how?"

"I know 'cause Willamina Redd-Grand told me! I had to find out from her!" Wanza screamed. "You know us Grand wives...we have to stick together. And she told me D-o-u-g had showed her your picture after you pulled a gun on the man on his wedding day. A gun, Money? A gun?!?"

"Well—"

"But it doesn't matter to me!" Wanza jumped in. "I wouldn't care if the two of y'all shot it out like it was the O-Kay Corral. Both of you liars deserve to be dead! Dead, I tell ya! Dead!"

"B-ut—" Money was getting a glimpse of that other, two-headed Wanza; the one that could make World War III look like a walk in the park. No hold bars. All gloves off—North Nashville style.

"And to think you had me thinking you were some kind of good guy." Wanza raged. "You been taking me out to dinner! You been sending me flowers! You even had me bragging about you to my Pastor! But I never would've fooled with you period...no how, no way...if I had o' *ever* known you were that *Man-Stealing* Melissa's brother!"

"B-ut—"

"Forget it!" Wanza marched around her desk. "You're a liar and a cheat, just like that conniving Douglas Grand. All you men are the same! Ain't none o' y'all to be trusted! You ain't worth two dead flies!" She fumed. "Well, I may not be nobody's first thought. But you betta believe I ain't gonna be nobody's after-thought!"

"B-ut—"

"I've been parading you in front o' Y." Wanza was flinging her hands around the room like a wild woman on steroids, while Money stood at attention with his back plastered to the wall. "I've had these young ladies at this Ministry snickering at me behind my back. And very well they should 'cause just like these silly girls, I let my heart...and what I wanted to see and wanted to feel...get in the way o' using my brain." She gasped for air. "'Cause while I've been preaching to them about finding a man who has a life plan that includes them, here I am letting a man *without* a plan get next to me. 'Cause I didn't even know yo real name!"

"Now hold it—"

"Naw! You hold it!" Wanza's face flared. "Even when Mrs. Lawson told me your full name...LaMont Mann—"

"Aww-now, don't go there!" Money finally protested. "I'd rather you kill me right here dead on the spot than call me by that name—"

"Even then," Wanza continued unrelentingly, "I didn't get it! And to think I took you into my confidence. I took you into my home." Wanza slowed pitifully, pushing back her angry tears. "I brought you around my boys...my boys...and I don't bring *no* man...*ever*...around my boys!"

"Are you done, yet?" Money pushed his back up off the wall. He was tired of waiting his turn to jump in like a kid playing double-dutch, and he was giving up hope that the wind would soon blow out of her sails.

"No, I'm not done!" Wanza reloaded, a little surprised at Money's reaction to her tirade. "You're the one that's done, Mister!" She blasted. "You get out o' here...and don't you *ever* show your face around here, again! Thank God, I didn't let you into my bed—"

"Aww-now, I could o' got in yo bed...all up in yo bed." Money wiggled his toothpick and gave her the soulful look he knew she couldn't resist. "But I couldn't let that happen until you knew Missy was my sister...and I just couldn't bring myself to tell ya—"

"And why not?"

"'Cause I didn't wanna lose you." Money's voice trembled with sincerity. "Don't you understand, Woman. The more I got to know you; the more I didn't wanna lose you—"

"Uh-huh?" Wanza's defenses wobbled badly.

"I was afraid," Money said truthfully. "I was afraid that if you knew Missy was my sister, you'd never wanna see me again—"

"You got that right!" Wanza rebounded on one sweet hip.

"And I was wrong." Money spread his arms out wide. "I should o' told you...back when we first met...but I was confused...confused about so many things—"

"And—"

"And for real-for real, I just didn't know what to do 'cause every time I saw you, Girl, I wanted to get with you—"

"Say what?" Wanza bobbled. Money's strong words and his frankness were striking a chord deep within her soul. And it was becoming clear to her that Money was the kind of man who loved hard, and the idea of losing her—before they could explore their true feelings—would've certainly been a scary proposition for him.

"You know," Money said quietly, "I really wanted Missy to be more like you—"

"Like me?" Wanza took a step back toward her chair.

"I wanted her to give that D-o-u-g just what you're giving me right now." Money chomped down hard on his toothpick. "I wanted her to tell him where to go, how far, how deep, and how wide." Money dropped his head. "I deserve this...and so did Doug. But Missy never would...she never did. I told her she didn't have to take everything that joker was putting down. I told her, 'I got yo back, Missy; don't go getting all nutty-brained 'bout this stuff. We're in this thing together.'" Money scrubbed his head between his hands. "But, maybe, I don't know...maybe, I protected her too much...she was so weak...and I tried to keep her safe from jokers like Doug—"

"But maybe she needed somebody bigger than you—"

"Whoa! Whatcha sayin'?" Wanza's words ripped through Money's pride like a chain saw. "Are you saying it wasn't my job to protect Missy—"

"Could be." Wanza jabbed. "Maybe, what she needed was a closer walk with Jesus—"

"But she had no real survival skills." Money explained. "She wanted to play the perfect family game with Doug, and she wouldn't say a mumbling word to the man to straighten him out. She just let him get away with everything. She even let him get away...with murder—"

"Murder?"

"Well, he murdered her self-esteem...her character...her dreams...and she just let him—"

"But this ain't about Melissa!" Wanza yanked hard on Money's chain. "This is about you and me."

"I know." Money gave her a cocky smile. "And that sounds real good to me; 'cause I'm peacock proud, Pretty Lady, to know that there is a you and me—"

"Quit that, Money." Wanza tried to resist his charms by flopping back into her chair. "You lied to me...or as good as...you should o' told me the truth...you should o' given it to me straight—"

"So you like it straight; do you?" Money teased.

"Quit that, Money Mann!"

"You're right; I should o' told you the truth from the start." Money raised his hands in surrender. "It was your right to know, so you could make up your own mind whether or not you wanted to be with me," he said, soulful eyes glimmering. "But...I've got even more truth to tell you now."

"What?" Wanza frowned, her fit of anger fast running out of steam. Money's direct eye contact and calm demeanor in the face of her fiery blasts was disarming. In her 'hood, Wanza had been known to bring gang-bangers to their knees when she unleashed on them, but Money didn't budge. And she knew if a man was unable or unwilling to break her code, he didn't deserve a shot at her heart. But here was Money, standing his ground and at least making the effort to see her point of view, which made him all the more endearing to her. *This boy right here is hangin' in there...and I've been rippin' him a new one!*

"You see, I am Missy's brother, true enough." Money took the chair across from Wanza's desk. "We've got the same mother...such as she was." Money slowed. He was having trouble wrapping his mind around his newfound status. "But Walter Mann...Pastor Walter Mann...is not my daddy."

"Say what?" Wanza gasped. She was now more interested in this juicy tidbit than Money's finagling with the truth.

"If you'll let me," Money said with the slightest wink, "I'll tell you all about it over dinner." He quickly added. "I am not trying to make light of your concerns, Wanza. You are exactly right. I just hope you'll find it in your heart to forgive me." He reached across the desk to hold her hands. "'Cause you are one-mo' fine looking woman, 'specially when you get that fire deep down in yo belly…umm-hmm." He flipped his toothpick like a swizzle stick and got his beg on. "And, Woman, I sho' do need you in my life—"

"Quit that, Money Mann!" Wanza smirked, but she didn't move her hands.

CHAPTER 18
The Mann Revelation

Money and Wanza had talked over dinner. In fact, their conversation had gone well into the night, but he was very unsure about where they'd left it. His lie about his identity had certainly put a wedge between them, and he wasn't sure if they'd ever be able to get past it. So the very next weekend, Money climbed back into his hoopty and took another trip to Knoxville. The kids were out of school for the summer and playing in the streets so he reminded himself to be cautious. And when he tapped on Sister Whatnot's door, she answered promptly.

"Why, hello, Money." She smiled. "Back so soon."

"Yes, ma'am," Money said, standing there like a little boy who'd lost his way.

"Did you come to discuss your letter from Hattie?"

"Yes, ma'am…that…and some other things…if you've got the time."

"Of course I have the time, young man. I'm retired." She giggled coquettishly. "Let's take our seats out on the porch, if that's alright with you. May I get you some refreshments?"

"No, ma'am" *None o' them nasty tea cakes…yuck!* "Thank you, though." Money said as he reclaimed the same seat he had on his first visit. He plopped down and buried his heavy head in his hands.

"What's wrong, Money?" Sister Whatnot said sweetly.

"There's this woman I like…and I think she likes me…but I've gone and messed it all up—"

"Why do you like this woman, Money?" Sister Whatnot inquired to be sure they were on the same page; that he was talking about qualities of substance and not just some romantic nonsense.

"I like what she stands for. I like the way she tries to help people. I like the way she stays true to her friends. I like the way she speaks her mind...even to me." Money's voice softened. "And I like the way the light falls on her cheeks when—"

"Okay." Sister Whatnot agreed before he drifted into their personal affairs. "You like this woman, Money. What happened?"

"You see, she just happens to be Douglas Grand's Wife #1—"

"Who?"

"And my sister, Missy, stole her husband away—"

"Oh?" Sister Whatnot wanted to be sure her mental scorecard was accurate. "So your sister became Wife #2?"

"Yes, ma'am." Money chomped down on his toothpick. "But when I met Wanza, I never told her that I was Missy's brother. I didn't tell her for fear it would ruin my chances—"

"Oh, what a tangled web we weave—"

"I know. I know all that." Money groaned. "I should o' told Wanza myself, but it just never seemed to be the right time—"

"And—"

"And...Wife #3...the current Mrs. Douglas Grand...believe it or not, she's friends with Wanza, too—"

"Oh?"

"Well, it's a long story...but Wife #3 let it slip who I am—"

"And Wanza was very annoyed—"

"Annoyed?" Money winced. "That woman pitched a fit! She tap danced all over my po' head! Hashtag #WorldWarIII! Hashtag #Ballistic!" Money slumped. "We kind o' talked a little since then, but I can feel her pulling back from me. I told her how it was when I was growing up. I told her why I was afraid to let her know who I really was. But I don't think she trusts me anymore. I just don't know what to think—"

"What do you do, Money?"

"Ma'am?"

"What is your employment?" Sister Whatnot clarified. "What do you do for a living?"

"Oh, that?" Money twirled his toothpick. "Well, I clean a number of downtown buildings…at night, mostly. Guess you could say I do janitorial work."

"Is that all you do?"

"Well, no." Money didn't know what she was driving at, but he played along. "I also volunteer at the Women's Services Center. I drive the van. I transport women and their kids over to Dipped in the Fire to get some help. That's how I met Wanza."

"Do you enjoy your job?"

"I mean…it's a job. It pays the bills."

"And the volunteer work for the Center; do you enjoy it?"

"Well, it's alright. Those women and their kids sho' need some help. And I guess it's the least I can do—"

"So is there anything else going on in your life?" Sister Whatnot tightened the noose.

"Well…I don't tell everyone this…but Missy did leave me a life insurance policy—"

"Oh?"

"Don't know if she forgot to sign it over to D-o-u-g when they married, or if she was just looking out for her big bro for a change…but, now, it's worth over…$800,000."

"Nearly a million dollars?" Sister Whatnot exhaled. "Now, that's a blessing! And what are you doing with your windfall?"

"Huh?"

"The money Melissa left you. What are you doing with it?"

"Oh, I've got it invested…but I don't ever touch it…I can't…it's like…blood money—"

"That's how you see it?"

"Yeah. Wouldn't you?"

"No, I would not," Mattie Whatnot said frankly. "My sister, Hattie, left me a sizeable inheritance, as well, but I don't consider it blood money. I consider it to be a gift of love with which she wanted to bless me; and I consider it to be mine to do with as I please."

"But—"

"So…if you could do anything in the world you pleased, what would you do, Money?"

"Well…I don't know." Money wiggled uncomfortably in his chair. "But I have always liked fast cars…fine cars. I guess I wouldn't mind owning or being part-owner of some kind o' foreign or classic car business." He resituated his toothpick. "I mean…now, wouldn't that be something? Vroom-Vroom!"

"Then why don't you do it, Money?" Sister Whatnot pinned him with her wise eyes. "You have the means—"

"But—"

"It seems to me that you've been marking time…paying penitence with your life…instead of living your life—"

"Ma'am?"

"You don't work at that janitorial job because you love it—"

"Love it? Ha!"

"That's exactly what I mean. Even though you have the means to transform your life, you stick with old habits…out of guilt…out of grief…I don't know. But you sat right here on this porch and repented of your past life; didn't you?"

"Yes, ma'am, I did—"

"Repentance is good. It's healthy. It's necessary that we agree with God about our sins. It helps us find our way back to Him. But when the Lord forgives us, he doesn't expect us to keep paying for our past, over and over again. He frees us for the purpose of moving on." Sister Whatnot sized him up. "And if Hattie's letter meant anything to you at all, Money—"

"It did." Money sat up straight. "'Cause now I know that coward, Walter Mann, was never my daddy—"

"So, now, it's time for you to move on with *your* life, and stop burying it under old, dead things."

"Yes, but—"

"You've been given the means to change your life, Money, and you refuse to do it." Sister Whatnot eyes squinted tightly. "How does that give God glory?"

"Oh—"

"You're still trying to pay a debt for which Jesus has already paid—"

"I never looked at it like that—"

"And you say you really like this woman, Wanza?"

"I do." Money lips curled into one of his bad-boy smiles. "I've seen that woman at her worst...and I still want more—"

"Well, it seems to me as if you've told her what happened in your past, but you've not shared with her your plans for your future." Sister Whatnot glimmered. "Being a woman, that's certainly something I'd be interested in hearing from you."

"You really think it would make a difference?"

"If you really care about this lady, Money—"

"I do—"

"Then go after her with all you've got," Sister Whatnot said encouragingly, like the Professor of Religion and Psychology she'd been for over 30 years. "She won't be able to see the real you until you stop bowing your present to your past...stop punishing yourself...stop paying this perpetual penitence by doing things you don't love. Stand up, Money...claim what's yours! Stand up, Money...live!"

CHAPTER 19
The Grand Scheme

It was shaping up to be a long, hot summer for Douglas Grand. His nose was so wide-open for Ryhema his business affairs had begun to slip—badly. He was trotting all over the globe trying to keep up with her. Wherever she was, that's where he wanted to be. Even his staff was growing weary of his constant neglect. Just that morning, Douglas had given his assistant, Chad, a tongue-lashing for missing a critical deadline in a service contract, but it was Douglas who'd forgotten to give him the order.

Since the start of his reckless obsession with Ryhema, the errors and miscues had started to mount, dating back to the time he'd missed his prime opportunity to make the dominoes fall in the Smooth Jazz community. At a critical juncture in the negotiations, Douglas had followed Ryhema's gig at Carnaval in Rio de Janeiro, Brazil, rather than attending the Smooth Jazz Festival in Cancun, Mexico. The staff he'd dispatched to the Festival to take his place was good—very good, in fact—but they didn't have his Midas touch for turning the major talent. Now, Douglas was left to start from scratch to restore their confidence in what he and Star Music Promotions International, Inc. had to offer. The misstep had leveled a devastating blow to Douglas' carefully crafted expansion plans.

On the heels of that fiasco, Douglas had also caught wind of a deal that he couldn't pass up. From the time he'd founded his company, he'd had it in his long-range plans to own a global recording/distribution business someday. That way, he could handle it all for his premier music clients. He could save them on recording fees, distribution fees, and not to mention, the wear and tear of flying all over the globe to record high quality music. With his studios flung out over the U.S. and the other countries in which he did business, Douglas could corner the market; cut out the middle man;

and swell the profits for Star, his stockholders, and more importantly, maximize his own personal wealth.

Douglas had heard it through the grapevine that Hickock Global Distribution had fallen on hard times. The head of the family empire, Papa Jude, had died, and his family was shaky. Papa Jude had assembled the ideal network, but his family was ill-equipped to sustain it. None of his sons had the business savvy needed to keep the enterprise afloat. In fact, Douglas had heard that they were already starting to sell off some of the international locations and the equipment, which made the network valuable. All the family seemed to care about was lining their own pockets with Papa Jude's cash. And with the shambles the family was making of the business, Douglas knew that if he didn't take bold steps to secure it, it wouldn't last out the year. *I've got to stop the bleeding!*

The only way Douglas could get the Hickock family to cease-and-desist their squandering ways was to meet their terms. Cash—his own personal cash—would have to be laid on the line over the next six months in order to keep the company solvent until Douglas could take the deal to his December Board meeting. Otherwise, Hickock would go on the chopping block to the highest bidder. But if he put up the $5-8 million of his own funds, which was needed to secure the option, by all accounts he could double his money in six months with this one acquisition. *This is the deal of a lifetime! And since I've been dropping the ball of late, I need a gimme to get me back on top o' my game...get my edge back.*

Unfortunately, Douglas would need the stockholder's votes to back his play at the December meeting. Since Star was now a publically-traded company, an acquisition of this type would require a change to the Board's charter, bylaws and company name in order to add the recording/distribution function to their portfolio. *Oh, for the good ol' days when I was my own boss!*

Moreover, Chad and his lawyers had cautioned Douglas about using his own millions to secure the Hickock deal. It was a risky proposition even though Douglas could expect to double his investment as a reward. The stakes were too high; the family was too shaky; and there were other sharks in the water circling the beleaguered company. Besides, with the December Board meeting being six months away, there was no guarantee that the Board would sanction the deal. And knowing what he knew about Douglas' and Ryhema's clandestine affair, Chad was uneasy about Willamina's loyalty to her husband at this point. "Douglas, if you go through with this Hickock deal," Chad warned, "you will *not* have enough ready cash to buy any more of your own company stock in Star Music Promotions." His green eyes pulsed like warning lights. "You'll be at the mercy…of your wife and her shares!"

"ENOUGH!" Douglas' voice boomed like a violent thunder clap, and Chad folded like a cheap suit, making a hasty exit. *What do they know?* Douglas meditated as he paced tight circles around the room. *They're just peons with a paycheck. They don't have my vision. This is my company! This is my deal! And I will get the votes I need…I must!*

Besides, as far as Douglas was concerned, he was in the clear with Willamina. There was no way for her to know about the millions he planned to invest in the Hickock deal. This was his money—his own personal earnings from the Fisk mega concert and the remains of Melissa's savings accounts. *The li'l sneak thief…she was stockpiling what she was skimming off the top from me!* And weeks before he'd recited his solemn wedding vows to Willamina, Douglas had stashed away his millions in an untraceable, off-shore account to prevent the prenup from ever turning against him. Shrewd businessman that he was, Douglas was all about covering his bets to protect his personal wealth and the continued solvency of his precious company. *Pretty Miss Redd will never get her hands on my millions…even if I decide to mess around with a side chick…or two.*

Consequently, Douglas had led his bride to believe that he'd plowed his personal earnings from the mega concert back into his business, and that was why he didn't have the ready cash to buy-up the majority of his company stock when the time came. But, in truth, Douglas saw Willamina as an opportunity. And it had always been his plan to access her millions to purchase the remaining shares he needed to put himself into the Chairman's seat so he wouldn't have to touch the nest egg he'd squirreled away in his hidden, off-shore account. But he never expected Willamina to beat him to the punch. In his wildest dreams, he never could've imagined that his lovely bride would purchase the stocks he needed as a wedding gift; and he certainly never anticipated she'd be holding his prized possessions in her name!

Nevertheless, Douglas knew the Hickock deal would be a cinch with his and Willamina's combined voting strength. Between them, they constituted the majority—51% of the voting shares. But therein lay the problem. Douglas was working overtime trying to appease Willamina and keep her in his camp. But he could sense his wife's growing frustration with his lack of physical and emotional closeness. He could sense her growing distrust of his exhausting, worldwide schedule. Because he was peeping and hiding with Ryhema, their marriage was hanging on by a slender thread, and he could feel it about to break. *And the madder she gets, the less I like her. I'm getting sick o' her and her hillbilly twang. She's starting to sound more and more like her crazy goat-roping cousins. And that's the problem with marriage…you never know whatcha gonna get 'til it's too late.*

Despite his feeble attempts—flowers, sweet notes, promises, and such—Douglas was fast running out of ways to repair the breach with Willamina before the December Board meeting. And at this critical juncture, he could ill-afford for his wife to catch on to his addiction to Ryhema. He could not afford for their marriage to breakdown. He could not afford for the prenup to kick-in. Being caught red-handed with Ryhema would mean losing power over the 21% voting shares that Willamina held in her hot little hands; the voting shares that he so desperately needed to make the deal of a lifetime with Hickock Global Distribution. And, now, with Ryhema in his heart and in his bed, Willamina's control over his voting shares was becoming a serious problem he needed to rectify...*ASAP! I cannot fail...I'll go belly-up...I'll be tapped out. But if I can get my hands on Willamina's shares...my troubles will be over...all over!*

The duplicity, the pretense, the constant shell game was starting to take a heavy toll on Douglas' psyche. He felt like a man caught in the middle of his own, hand-crafted nightmare. The drums of doom that had been banging at the back of his skull were getting progressively louder. He'd gotten himself into this mess, and, now, he had to find a way out. *And desperate men must take desperate measures.*

Douglas had hoped that his scheme to throw Essex and his wife together in a steamy, sordid love affair would do the trick. The prenup would kick-in—in his favor—and that would be that. But his plan seemed to have backfired, and Essex appeared to have an even higher regard, a grander level of respect for Willamina than ever before. He treated her like she was a queen, and he was her loyal subject. Even Douglas' hush-hush private detective had failed to turn up any dirt on his Christian-hearted wife and Essex—or any other man, for that matter—and Douglas was getting desperate. He needed to put an end to his charade of a marriage to *Pretty Miss Redd*—and come out whole, free, and very rich in the process. *I need her to disappear...poof...so I can get on with my life with Ravishing Ryhema...the only woman I have ever truly loved.*

CHAPTER 20
The Grand Plot

The summer was heating up for Essex, as well. He'd noticed the growing strain on Douglas' face and his haggard appearance, but said nothing. It was none of his concern. He was more concerned with figuring out who seemed to be following him and why. It wasn't an everyday occurrence; if it had been, he would have ferreted out the stalker by now. No, it was so sporadic that even Essex, with his Delta Force skills, could not nail it down. A few times, he'd gotten the feeling of being watched while driving Willamina in the Bentley. But most of the time, he'd get the sensation when he was transporting Douglas and Ryhema in the Rolls, or he'd feel eyes on him when he was stationed near Douglas' downtown offices. It was a raw, gnawing feeling, and Essex was becoming extremely frustrated. At any given moment, he would sense a tail on him that he was unable to shake.

One time in particular, when Douglas and Ryhema were stashed in their favorite hideaway—the Hotel Carlisle—Essex had tried to set a trap for the stalker. He parked the Rolls in the valet parking area and under the cover of darkness, he stealthily double-backed down the other side of the street. He had his Sig Sauer pistol at the ready, but he only saw two regular citizens going and coming on the sidewalk. An old man with a long, gray beard, dressed in pressed overalls and walking his anemic-looking dog was at one end of the sidewalk. And at the other, a scraggly-headed bum was stumbling along, wailing some but-awful Blue Grass tune about being 'a man of constant sorrows', while he was checking all the trash cans for the scraps rich people left behind.

Essex didn't bother mentioning his suspicions to Douglas. The man was too totally distracted by his lustful globetrotting to notice much else. He'd seen the goings on in the backseat of the Rolls between Douglas and Ryhema, and it looked like it was getting more and more serious. Essex had also spotted the *Rock of Gibraltar*—a mega 10 carat diamond—that Douglas had placed on the ring finger of the young lady's left hand, and it made him slightly nervous. *Should I break confidence and tell Miz G?* But instead of letting it add to his worries, Essex merely kept a closer watch on Willamina to be sure he kept her safe.

"Essex, my man!" Douglas came up from behind, startling him in the office parking lot.

"Yes, Boss." Essex grunted, resisting the natural urge to jump.

"Get in and let's ride."

"Sure thing." Essex hopped into the driver's seat and revved up the engine.

Once he'd settled into the passenger compartment of the Rolls, Douglas cleared his throat and opened the tinted partition. "Say there, Essex," he said almost jovially, "got a question for you."

"Shoot."

"That's closer to the point than you realize." Douglas snorted. "You see, I've got this friend...and he's in the market...for a good hit man—"

SCREECH!

"Watch your driving, man!" Douglas yelped as he almost took a tumble in the rear seat.

"Hit man?!?" Essex flapped, regaining his footing on the gas pedal of the Rolls.

"Well...I don't quite know how to put it." Douglas confessed, resituating himself in the plush passenger compartment. "But he's my friend, you see...and well...he's in the market for a good hit man—"

"Why does your friend need such a man?" Essex's voice sizzled. "Sounds like a permanent solution to a problem that may be only temporary—"

"Well, he's gotten in over his head…with the mob…and they're threating his life…and that of his family," Douglas said convincingly. "And he…my friend…he needs to put some distance between himself and those goons—"

"Fight fire with fire, heh?" Essex mused aloud.

"Something like that." Douglas quibbled. "Got anybody in mind?"

"Yeah…there is this one guy in NOLA; goes by the name of John R. He can surely handle your troubles…your friend's troubles…for a price, that is."

"Well, if you think he's trustworthy enough to get the job done, maybe he can handle it…my friend's problem, I mean."

"Let us just say, John R., he is no amateur." Essex snorted. "There are quite a few unmarked graves in Potter's Field at this man's hands."

"Sounds promising." Douglas wiggled anxiously in his seat. "Can you get me his number…to give to my friend?"

"It does not work like that, Mizter G. You'll have to give me your friend's number to give to John R."

"Nope." Douglas' voice tensed. "That can't happen. My friend wants to stay in the shadows on this."

"Tell you what then, Mon." Essex obliged. "I'll get you an untraceable, prepaid cellphone from one of the Asian stores…to give to your friend…and I will give John R. the number. He will get in touch with your friend…that is, if he is interested in taking the job."

"Sounds like a long way 'round—"

"John R. does not know you…or your friend…and you do not know him…that is the way he will want to keep it."

"How much do you think it'll cost?"

"That will undoubtedly depend on the job," Essex said. "But he will undoubtedly want half up front and half after the job is finished. Tout de suite."

"Right away, huh?"

"Yes."

"Sounds convoluted to me." Douglas shook his head. "But I'll pass the info on…to my friend—"

"You do that." Essex declared.

"And what do we do if he wants to go forward?"

"We?" Essex queried.

"Yes." Douglas bobbled badly. "He's a real good friend…and I want to put him on the right track."

"If he desires to go forward, there will be no turning back." Essex shifted in his seat. "But we can get your friend the proper phone. I will give John R. the number. Your friend can take it from there, Mizter G."

"Sounds like a plan." Douglas intoned. "Need to get this done right away…and get out of the middle as soon as possible." *And kill two birds with one stone, so to speak. I'll get Willamina's shares for my Hickock deal…and as an extra-added bonus, I'll get Ravishing Ryhema, too!*

"Sure. Sure thing," Essex said convincingly. But given his track record, he didn't trust Douglas Grand as far as he could throw a fat elephant. So he'd be keeping his eyes and ears open from now on. He certainly hoped this had nothing to do with Miz G, but if it did he'd be willing to give his very life for that fine woman. If it ever came to it, he'd certainly be willing to put his body between her and a bullet.

CHAPTER 21
The Redd Cloud

When Essex pulled up across the street from the Yang Wig Emporium, he glimpsed a pork-faced man exiting the car that had parked two cars behind him. When Essex came out of the wig shop with the untraceable, pre-paid cellphone, he spied the portly, pork-faced gent trying to duck behind the corner of the building. But his attempt at an evasive move was just a little too slow. His belly was still exposed.

Essex sped around the corner and collared the man. "Who are you; and why are you tailing me?" Essex squeezed the fat man's collar.

"Ahh...c'mon now, Son." The man was turning beet red as he strained to speak. "You...you got me all wrong—"

"Talk...and talk fast!" Essex massive hands shook him loose while taking his Sig Sauer out of its shoulder holster.

"My name's Jeb," the fat man stuttered and pointed to the scraggly-headed driver of his car that was sneaking up on Essex from the rear. "And this here's my cousin, John Earl," he said, as his red neck wiggled. "And we's Willamina Redd's kin."

"You are what?" Essex growled, unconvinced. Although, he did recognize the one who'd posed as the scraggly-headed bum with a penchant for singing Blue Grass tunes on side streets. But he couldn't believe this wretched pair could be any relation to his queen. "Show me some I.D."

"Okay. Okay." Both of the men rambled into their back pockets and pulled out tattered wallets.

"Let me see." Essex snatched the driver's licenses from their shaking hands.

"Jeb Redd. Texas." Essex read aloud, while keeping a close watch on the slippery pair. "Jonrenacious Redd?" Essex grumbled. "Okay. I will stick with John Earl."

"Jes bet you will." The two mountain men snickered.

"So let us go over this again." Essex growled. "Why are you following me?"

"We ain't following you none, so to speak." Jeb quibbled. "We's following that no-count husband o' her'n."

"What do you want from Mizter G?" Essex quizzed.

"We don't want nuttin' from the man or care nuttin' 'bout his doings." Cousin Jeb raved. "All we cares about is Cousin Willamina! 'Cause we aims to be sho' that he don't leave her no mo' worse off than the day he found her."

"He can go to blazes for all we care!" John R.'s glass eye blinked out each word."

"I care about Miz G, too." Essex eased up. "She is a wonderful lady—"

"She is that." The two men chanted. "She's our kin, and we goes all out for our kin."

"So the two of you have been following me all this time?"

"Well, yeah…us…and the rest o' the boys—"

"The boys? How many?"

"Well…there's…uhh—"

"Never mind!" Essex snapped. He didn't have the kind of time it would take for him to count them all up on his quivering fat fingers.

"But we ain't been tracking you all the time," Jeb explained, "jes here and there…jes us wanting to keep our eyes open and our ears to the ground—"

"And there are things happening." Essex looked down at the untraceable phone he was holding. "Things are in the making that I do not understand, but—"

"But?" Cousin Jeb prompted. "But what?"

126

"Like I say—" Essex slowed. "I do not understand, yet. But I am keeping my eyes and ears open, as well, to keep Miz G safe."

"Safe?" Jeb blustered. "Is the girl in some sort o' danger?"

"I do not know." Essex exhaled. "But I am beginning to think the two of you can be trusted—"

"Trusted?" Jeb protested. "Course we can be trusted...where Willamina's concerned. But I wouldn't trust this one here 'round a full jug of corn whiskey." Jeb jabbed John Earl in the side.

"It is all as I say." Essex ignored their ramblings. "And I will tell you what it is I will do."

"What? What?"

"Give me your telephone numbers, and I will give you mine." Essex offered. "And if I need you, I will call you—"

"And if you needs us," Jeb said, stepping up to the plate, "we'll be right there on the double."

"Sounds like a plan," Essex said pointedly. "And in the meantime, the two of you can *stop* following me—"

"You got it! And you need not worry none." Jeb vowed. "When we handles a thang, it's handled—"

"And they won't find hide-nor-hair of 'em up in them-thar hills." John Earl spoke up, uncharacteristically, and it was Jeb's turn to provide the echo.

"No, siree...not hide-nor-hair!" Jeb chanted and unleashed one of his piercing wolf howls. "Whoo-Whoo-Whoo!"

CHAPTER 22
The Mann Plan

It was approaching the dog-days of summer in Nashville when Money invited Wanza to lunch at the Howlin' Moon Blues Café; the restaurant that he and Missy once frequented. Wanza accepted his invitation—reluctantly. When they were finally settled in their booth and the waiter had come and gone, there was no stopping Money. He went straight to the point.

"Wanza," he said, "I guess I never told you that Missy left me a li'l coin." He snapped on his toothpick. "But I've been so busy feeling guilty, and angry, and sorry for myself, I never gave it much thought. But I've been talking to Sister Whatnot—"

"Who?" Wanza puzzled at the name that sounded like somebody from the psychic hotline.

"She's the lady from my hometown; remember? Long story." Money shrugged. "But anyhoo, I've come up with an action plan; something that's been long overdue. 'Cause a man without a plan is like a heavyweight fighter with something to prove. He can't be satisfied 'til he gets the job done."

"Wow!" Wanza teased. "You came up with that line all by yourself, huh?"

"Yep." Money didn't let her wisecrack sway him off point. "I've always been into cars, you know…fast cars, high-priced cars, classic cars. So I got me some lawyers, and we're making a deal with Nashville Prestige Imports…and I'm gonna be part owner of the finest foreign car dealer in Brentwood—"

"Oh, really?" Wanza sized-up the man sitting across the table from her like she was seeing him for the first time.

"Yep." Money continued. "And I'm also buying an interest in Classic Cars of America. That way, I can rebuild and show my own remakes on the classic car circuit. We're going after it big-time. We're gonna get some national sponsors and—"

"And you're pretty excited, huh?" Wanza was spellbound. She'd always liked Money, for reasons even she didn't understand; but, now, she was seeing him as a man with a plan. She nibbled at her spicy chicken quesadillas while Money's favorite mushroom cheeseburger sat untouched.

"And I got rid o' my old hoopty, too, so I can ride you around in style." Money slid over his key fob that bore the four distinctive rings of Audi.

"A new car, too?"

"Yep, I'm juiced!" Money twirled his toothpick. "I've talked it over with the Lord, and I'm more sure of the course I'm taking in my life than ever before."

"Oh, Money." Wanza gave him a genuinely warm smile. "I am so happy for you. Really!"

"And I've decided to quit volunteering at the Center." Money twisted his lips into a wry smile. "So I can devote more time to my business interests…and help you out at Dipped in the Fire…whenever you need me."

"Sounds like you've given your plans a lot of serious thought, Money—"

"Yep, but none of it matters, Wanza…none of it—" Money said, reaching across the table to touch her hand. "If I don't have you."

"Me?"

"Girl, don't you know I've been trying to tell you I love you all this time?" Money's soulful eyes dipped into their sockets like golden sunsets. "I love you, Wanza." He squeezed her hands like a protective glove. "And I wanna spend the rest of my natural-born days with you."

"Mon-ey," Wanza stammered, at a loss for words. "But you lied to me—"

"I know, and I'm sorry, Baby. And I swear I'll never do it again—"

"But I have two boys I dearly love. I have a job that I'm pouring my heart into. Do you think we really could?"

"Don't you get it, Woman? I wanna be with you ride-or-die, up-or-down. I love you, Wanza…just like you are." Money resolved. "You can do and be whatever you want, but I want you to do it and be it with me."

"Oh, Money, I'm so proud of you—"

"And we don't have to live in that big ol' mansion on Legends Way if you don't want to. Me, you, and the boys…we can live wherever you say—"

"Oh, Money!" Wanza was breathless. "And I love you, too…I really do! I was attracted to you based on your charming personality." Wanza admitted grudgingly. "But I fell in love with you based on your character." She gushed. "I love the way you love, Money…so fierce, and faithful, and true…even when you're in pain…the way you loved Melissa—" Wanza changed over to Money's side of the booth and planted a blazing kiss on his lips. "But you know us 'round-the-way gurrls; we go at it hard—"

"Baby, I invented hard." Money's voice mellowed into the warmth of a summer's evening. He returned her kiss with the passion of a thousand lifetimes, pulling her down into the depths of his longing fire.

"Whew!" Wanza said, coming up for air. "Then I'm glad you chose a plan that includes ole-Wanza—"

"You better bet it does." Money squeezed her warm, sexy body close to his. "'Cause ole-Money *needs* himself some Wanza."

CHAPTER 23

The Grand Slam

"Come in. Come in." Ryhema scanned the long hallway as she snatched Willamina into the Grand Bridal Suite at the Waldorf Astoria Hotel in downtown Nashville. It was a hot night in September. She'd booked the suite because she thought it would be the last place anyone would expect to find the two of them together—especially, Douglas Grand. But little did Ryhema know that this is where Douglas and Willamina had spent their spectacular wedding night together.

"Howdy." Willamina walked in slowly, like she was entering into a sacred place. "You said you needed to see me...lickety-split?"

"Yes." Ryhema's voice cracked. "It is urgent."

"Okay...you got me—"

"Did anyone see you in the lobby?" Ryhema buzzed. "Or in the elevator? Did Essex drive you over?"

"Nope." Willamina's voice tightened. "I drove myself over here, and I made sure nobody spotted me in the lobby downstairs 'cause I don't wanna be seen in here anymore than you do. So what's this all about?"

"Can I get you something to drink...eat?" Ryhema rocked on her five-inch heels.

"No." Willamina was starting to get annoyed. "Let's just get down to brass tacks; shall we?"

"Well...I asked you here Willamina...can I call you Willamina?"

"What else you gon' call me, Girl?" Willamina's nerves were sharpening the edges on her native tongue. "What is it you want? Spit it out—"

"Well, I asked you here." Ryhema's heart was pounding like a startled bird's. "Because my Granny came to me in a dream—"

"Yo who?"

"Just hear me out…please." Ryhema pleaded and offered her guest a seat on the white leather sofa.

"Alright." Willamina agreed to sit beside her, but wasn't yet quite sure if she was dealing with a mad woman.

"I've been having this terrible pain." Ryhema began. "Pain that came at me out of nowhere…excruciating, mind-numbing pain…hit me like a bullet train." She sniffed. "And it all started about the time…about the same time…I started having an affair with your husband—"

"Say what?!?" Willamina nearly shouted, and her body rose up six inches off the sofa. "What're you sayin' to me?"

"Please, sit down, Willamina, and hear me out. Please." Ryhema's pretty eyes were starting to glaze over with worry. Maybe, this hadn't been such a good idea after all. Willamina had her by about 50 pounds, and the look in her eyes was saying she was prepared to go to war.

"I'll give you two minutes to explain yo'self, Miss Lady." Willamina exclaimed. "And boy-howdy it betta be good!"

"You see," Ryhema said, tripping over her hurried words, "my Granny came to me in a dream. And she said, 'Ryhema, you ain't gonna never get rid o' that pain in your body 'til you do right by Willamina Grand and stop sleeping with her husband.'" She mimicked her grandmother's grave tone. "My Granny was a big fan o' yours before she died last year." Ryhema added. "And my Granny…she ain't never been wrong."

"Go 'head." Willamina's jaws were clenched so tightly they were starting to crackle.

"Well…I've been having an affair with Douglas since my Paris gig back in the spring—"

"What?!?" Willamina yelped when she remembered how Douglas had turned her down for their honeymoon trip to France. "Douglas…came to see you…in Paris?"

"And I had no intentions of getting involved with your husband," Ryhema said solemnly. "But I looked up in Paris, and there he was. The man had made me millions. How could I deny him one night? Isn't that how business is done in this industry? Don't big men in the business expect those kinds of perks?" Ryhema pulled out a piece of gum and started to chew. "I don't drink or swear," she said, "but I chew gum when I get nervous." Her words had started flowing like a fountain. "But now…Douglas like…he turns up at all my gigs…wherever I am…seems like your husband is obsessed with me…or stalking me…or something. It's creeping me out! And I never…not in a million years…not ever… expected Douglas to fall in love with me." She smacked on her gum. "He says he loves me. He says he's never said those three words to another woman in his life and meant it." Ryhema flashed her *Rock of Gibraltar* at Willamina—the 10-carat diamond that Douglas had placed on the ring finger of her left hand. "He says he wants to marry me!"

"Marry you?!?" In that moment, Willamina's heart shattered like it was one of the golden chandeliers that had presided over their lavish wedding reception less than a year before. But since their wedding night in this very room, Douglas had been less than amorous toward her. He was always claiming to be too busy; or too tired; or working on expansion plans to grow his empire and make his shareholders even more outrageous profits; or he was not at home at all. And his string of out-of-town trips was starting to make more sense to her now; they probably mirrored Ryhema's concert schedule.

Sure, Willamina had her own share of gigs all over the country that kept her away from home, but that was business and that was their deal going into the marriage. But she was always ready and willing to resume her intimacy with her husband when she returned. But none of Douglas' advances to her had ever compared to the lovemaking, the openness, the all-consuming fire that they'd tasted on that one splendid night together. The fiery passion that they'd shared in this bed in this hotel room had fizzled into a tepid, lackluster performance in their own bedroom.

"But I don't want to marry Douglas!" Ryhema startled her back to the present. "I don't want to marry your husband!" She cried. "He's an alright guy, but he's too…too old for me. I want my own family…my own husband…my own home. I don't even know if Douglas can give me kids, or if he's too old to want kids." Ryhema wrung her dainty, bejeweled hands. "Oh, I should've listened to Cosmos—"

"Cosmos?" Willamina flickered. "You know Cosmos Cordell?"

"Of course." Ryhema spouted. "Everybody knows Cosmos. He tried to get me to sign with him before Douglas, but Douglas offered me way more money and way more gigs. But Cosmos said I didn't need to be a star right away…stars burn out too fast. He offered me an opportunity to build a solid career from the ground up…the kind that could last a lifetime. With my talent, Cosmos said I could stay beautiful like Tina; adored like Bey; and immortal like Sade." Ryhema felt herself drifting off course. "So…you know Cosmos, too?"

"Of course, I do" Willamina clipped. "He used to be my equipment manager back-in-the-day when he first started out in the business. But he wanted to go out on his own…be a music promotor…so I bankrolled him 'til he could get his feet under him. But he's quite successful in his own rights, now, and he's paid me back a thousand times over."

"When you were backing him, must've been around the same time I first met him." Ryhema deduced. "I really liked him, you know…in more ways than one. He's around my age…and oh, so cute." She drifted. "But there was Douglas, waving all those millions in front of my face, and I just couldn't turn him down. I am a material girl, you know—"

"Go figure—"

"But being a star ain't about nothing!" Ryhema resituated her aching bottom. "We've got all these kids thinking we're so special and thinking they can make big money without having to work for it. But this is work...this is hard work and just so many people can get to the top. And it has less to do with talent and more to do with promotion...that's why I picked Douglas over Cosmos. But I was wrong. I should've listened to Cosmos...and I should've listened to my Granny, too. 'You ain't never gonna stop hurtin' with another woman's husband in your bed.'"

"Uh-huh." Willamina hissed. "So you say."

"Despite what you might think of me, Miss Willamina, I *was* raised right." Ryhema whined. "I know people accuse me of performing...nearly naked...and I'm so glad my Granny's not here to see me...but if I don't do it, somebody will. And I've got to keep my name out there. I've got to stay in the public's eye or my star will surely flame out. But there's so much of this life I didn't ask for and don't want, but I'm caught and I can't see my way clear...and this pain...this gut-wrenching pain just won't let up. This daily, chronic pain is eating me up like a monster. It's taking all the spark outta my life. I can't think! I can't feel! I can't sing!" Ryhema was bouncing her knees frantically trying to stave off the pain starting to poke through her meds.

"My doctor says it's sciatica, or bursitis, or piriformis, or some other devilish inflammation, but I can't perform unless I take the oxy he prescribes. But I don't wanna be some pill-popping, oxy-fiend. So I try to hold off on the pills until I perform, but I just cannot stand this pain...not any longer." Her splendid face crumbled mournfully.

"And Douglas…Douglas…he doesn't care about my pain…he just wants what he wants!"

Ryhema broke down in wretched sobs. "I'm sorry Miss Willamina…so very sorry…I'm sorry I ever slept with your husband." She cried. "But believe me…I don't want your husband. I don't wanna marry your husband. I just want my life back! I just want this pain to stop! Please. Please, Willamina, say you forgive me. Please say it so this pain will go away!"

"Now, you calm down, Chile". The break in Willamina's heart was equal to the colossal crack in her marriage vows, but she couldn't help feeling sorry for this fragile young lady. "So tell me…what is it you really want?"

"I wanna leave Douglas," Ryhema said without hesitation. "I wanna get back with Cosmos. I wanna do what Cosmos said…build my career…from the bottom up…if it's not too late—"

"Too late?" Willamina had to smile at this 25 year-old super star who was about to give up on life because her dear husband, Douglas Grand—a grown man of over 40—couldn't keep it in his pants. And she was beginning to think that there was a definite pattern to all his schemes and subterfuge—first Essex and now Ryhema. And it had everything to do with Douglas getting from under. *That blasted prenup*! "No, it's not too late, Ryhema." Willamina reassured her. "We can talk to Cosmos…together…if you want."

"Yes, please." Ryhema perked up a bit. "So you do forgive me, Willamina…please say you forgive me."

Willamina drew in a deep cleansing breath and blew it out. Anybody watching would have seen the white-hot smoke it produced. "No, I can't say how's I forgive you, not just yet." She clenched her fingers together, resisting the urge to climb this young girl like a pine sapling and do her bodily harm. *Like I did Betty Jo Reeker that time in the third grade…for having the nerve to call my mama ugly!*

But deep in her heart-of-hearts she knew this affair couldn't have gotten to this fever-pitch without Douglas' insistence. "But I am a far piece better off to getting there since we've had this li'l talk." Willamina admitted. Then she stood and headed for the door before she changed her mind about giving this girl the beat down of her life. "You spend the night here, Suga. Get yourself rested up some. And I'm going home."

"You won't tell Douglas I told you all this…any o' this…will you?" Ryhema knew she had the right to be fearful, because she'd seen how ruthless Douglas could be when he'd been crossed by people he'd trusted. She'd seen the fire in his eyes when poor Chad made the slightest scheduling error, even when it was Douglas who was at fault. She also knew him to take great pleasure in sudden, unexpected cruelties, like the time he'd dumped the frigid remains of the ice bucket all over her sore, naked body when she'd finally summoned up the courage to tell him she wanted out.

"Tell Douglas?" Willamina red lips curled into a rueful smile. "No chance o' that, Li'l Lady…no chance o' that a-tall." She headed for the door before stopping dead in her tracks. Slowly, she swiveled toward Ryhema and said, "I sincerely hope your pain goes away, now, Suga, and I hope your Granny will let you have some sweet dreams tonight. Because all in all, I do…I forgive you…for Jesus' sake." She swung back her long, red curls. "And I thank you for letting me know where I stand in my own house. 'Cause Jesus is just keeping His promise to me…there ain't nothing hid that won't be revealed." Willamina pulled hard on the door knob, but she couldn't resist her last chance to throw a little shade. "And it might do yo pain some good if'n you get yo'self outta them five-inch heels." She jabbed as she closed the door behind her. "Sweet dreams, Suga."

CHAPTER 24
The Mann Union

It was a warm first Friday in October when the whole thing went down. An odd band of folk joined hands and prayed in Nashville's Davidson County Courthouse. In attendance were Pastor and Mrs. Clarence Meadows; Sister Mattie Whatnot; Yteesha Seereta Lee; Willamina Redd-Grand; and, of course, the bride and groom—Money and Wanza. Wanza's boys, Derek and Donovan Grand, were also there to round out the motley crew. But before they prayed, Money sought out the nearest trash bin and tossed in his trademark toothpick—for good. *I don't need this crutch no mo.*

The happy couple was dressed casually and comfortably. There were no frills or fanfare planned; none needed. The fireworks were in their hearts, and they didn't want any more time to pass until they could be together. *I have found whom my soul loveth.* So when Money and Wanza exchanged their solemn vows before the Justice of the Peace, their devoted love and commitment to each other reigned supreme over the entire gathering. The placing of simple, black tungsten wedding bands on each other's fingers sealed their unbreakable promise.

After the ceremony, the boys held onto their mom and Money real tight. They wanted a dad. They needed one. And after they'd shared hugs, tears and kisses, Y whisked them off to pick up her two from pre-school.

"I've got to run, too," Willamina said when she was able to pull Money and Wanza aside. "I've got a gig in Las Vegas this weekend."

"Wow!" Wanza intoned. "You do get around."

"Well, I've gotta get out there and promote my new single. It's been nominated for an award in December." Willamina tried to add some sparkle to her smile. "But I wanted the two of you to have this." She handed them a gold-embossed envelope with the newlyweds names scrolled in sprawling calligraphy. "But I want you to promise me you won't open it 'til after your honeymoon down in Florida. You'll understand…and I really do hope the very best for y'all." *The same hope I had for me and Douglas this time last October…but now—*

"We promise." Money and Wanza vowed in unison. "We're taking the boys with us. They've always wanted to go to Disneyworld."

Money made it a priority to walk over and shake Pastor Meadows' hand. "Thank you, Pastor, for coming," he said. "Wanza thinks very highly of you."

"And it's been my unique pleasure to have Wanza as a member of my flock." Pastor Meadows smiled.

"Pastor, I just want you to know," Money continued, "I realize I need a church home. And when me, Wanza and the kids get back from Disneyworld, we're coming to True Vine…as a family."

"God bless you, Son." Pastor Meadows clapped him on his back. "It's so good to see a man step-up and take the lead for his family. I know Wanza and the boys will be very pleased."

Since Sister Whatnot had taken the Greyhound bus up from Knoxville, she was preparing to make her return trip when Candi Meadows stepped in. "There's no way we're going to let you ride that bus back to Knoxville," she said. She'd taken an immediate liking to Sister Whatnot. The love in their spirits had drawn the two women together. "Clarence and I would love to take you to lunch, and we'd be delighted to drive you home when you're ready. Isn't that right, Clarence?"

"Of course, dear; sure thing." The pastor agreed. "I'd love to take the ride down to Knoxville and have a look around."

"I'll accept," Sister Whatnot said in her quiet way, "only if you'll agree to stop over at my home for dinner."

"We'd love to," Candi Meadows said joyfully.

"Then it's settled." Pastor Meadows added.

"Just a moment." Sister Whatnot excused herself from the Meadows with a sweet smile and approached the newlyweds.

"I love you, Money and Wanza." Sister Whatnot encircled the happy couple in her arms. "And I know everything is going to be alright. Always put your trust in the Lord, and He will make the way for you. Is that understood?"

"Yes, ma'am." Money nodded, and Wanza returned her warm hug. "Thank you so much for coming to be with us. It was really nice to meet you," Wanza said.

"It was like having Mother Whatnot by my side." Money's soulful eyes tumbled, and Mattie Whatnot understood. She leaned in close and squeezed his tattooed hands.

CHAPTER 25
The Mann Code

Two weeks after their honeymoon at Disneyworld, Money kept a promise to his bride. It was on a November evening, and the chill of fall was in the air. Wanza kept her place in the background at the Orientation Meeting, but her heart was brimming over with love.

"Greetings, Ladies." Money gave the roomful of young ladies at Dipped in the Fire Ministries a crooked, bad-boy smile. "Guess you've heard it through the grapevine by now that me and Wanza, here, got married," he said through a barrage of applause, whistles and catcalls. "And I'm the happiest man in the world." His old-soul eyes misted. "But you also probably know I ain't always been no good guy. In fact, I'm that bad boy you all love." Money gave them a devilish wink. "I've been in these hard streets. I did my dirt. And I paid my debt to society." Money rolled up his sleeves to expose all of his prison ink. "I went to jail." The room hushed.

"But I also love the Lord." Money quickly confessed. "So my wife, Mrs. Wanza Johnson-Mann, asked me to give you the benefit of what I know to be true about men in hopes that it'll help you make better choices…and help you build yo life plan on solid ground for you and yo children. So I ain't talking to you tonight as a pastor or some teacher…or even the preacher's kid that I am…I'm talkin' to you as yo boy, Ole-Money. You feel me?" The roomful of ladies gave him a serious, concerted nod. "Now, I'm gonna keep this brief 'cause I ain't no talker." Money looked at his bride with loving eyes. "That's Wanza's department. But since she asked me to give you a sneak peek into the top secret *Mann-Code Playbook*…well, here we go."

"First: Find a man with a plan. If a man doesn't have at least a semi-clear direction that he's trying to move his future toward…financially or family-wise…then he's probably not in the head-space to want a wife." Money wiggled his index finger. "And if his conversation ain't workin' for you…if it ain't including you and yo kids…cut it off." Money breathed a sigh of relief as he recalled his last *come-to-Jesus* meeting with Sister Whatnot that had gotten him on the right track with his beloved Wanza. "Besides," he said, "when a man steps to you without a plan, what he's sayin' is: 'Gimme everything you've got…yo time, yo body, yo future, yo dignity…but I ain't gonna give you nothing in return.' And that's messed up 'cause love is what it does! Feel me?"

Money held up two fingers. "Second: Find a man who likes responsibility. If you notice he goes out of his way *not* to accept responsibility for things and wants to keep everything *light*, he probably doesn't understand that growth and the important things in life are only gained by going after 'em hard."

Money raised three fingers. "Third: Listen to what he says about himself. If he tells you he's not ready to be serious, or get married, or have kids, etc., then he is not. Don't try to change his mind. Because *kickin-it*…only helps the man be as loose and carefree as he wants to be. But it doesn't help you. It doesn't help you to establish a home and protection for you and yo kids. You've gotta have a vision or a view of what you want your life to look like. And if a man's not bringing that to the table, you don't need him. Most men just like having access, so they can move in and out at will. But everything and everybody ain't looking out for you and yo best interest. You've got to do that for yo'self." Money cocked his head sharply to one side. "And you don't need no *Suga-Daddies* just to help you pay yo bills, neither. That's why you're here…working so hard…'cause you're learning how to pay yo own bills. Right?"

142

Money shrugged as he heard the quiet groans from his audience. "Okay, I'll admit it. Sex adds color to the black and white. But it's the black and white you've gotta live with. And if it ain't right for ya, the sex won't be good to ya...at least, not for long. Besides, sex doesn't mean *love* to men, but stepping up to the plate to marry you and take care of you and yo kids; now, that's love."

Money gave the ladies a wide grin as he watched his words sinking in. Then he continued. "Ok...so those are the three major ones. But here're three more quickies from yo ole-boy, Money." He ticked them off quickly.

"One: Don't kiss a man you're not planning to marry. Most men know if they can kiss you...let's just say, they can get you to go all the way." Money didn't let their guilty giggles deter his resolve.

"Two: Don't be caught dead with a man by yo'self after 10 o'clock at night." Money winked. "For whatever reason, Ladies, midnight is the bewitching hour. I'll just leave that one right there with ya." He slowed.

"And Three," he said, "'cause I always save the best for last. Do not bring any man...no man...around yo kids that you're not planning to marry. Yo children do not need any mo *uncles*. A man is not gonna look out for you unless he wants to marry you...so you've gotta look out for yo'self...and for yo kids. A man will give his life for what he values...and walk away from what he don't." Money snuck a peak at Wanza and gave her the kind of smile that always made her weak in the knees "*You* are the prize...so don't play yo'self cheap. Right after God...love yo'self and yo children first."

Money felt his preach coming on as he remembered Missy, and in some ways, pitied his own unfortunate mother. "If a man don't wanna be seen with you in public; won't take you around his friends; won't give it to you straight; won't give you his time; and won't pay yo way, he ain't the one for you. And he don't need a *taste* to see if he wants the whole package. A man in love can always make his

143

woman's body sing." Money slowed. "You can't *win* a man's heart," he said. "He has to *earn* your heart. Giving yourself away won't make him love you. In fact, it might make him despise you. A real man wants to step-up...so always give him less than you receive." Money choked-up over the woeful faces on the beautiful young mothers who were going it alone. "That's it for me, Ladies." He raised his two fingers symbolically. "Peace-Out!"

"Oh...and one more thing." Money quickly doubled-back to the podium with a word of encouragement while the young women were catching their collective breath. "Don't be disappointed at what you've done up until now, or what someone else has done to you," he said. "People mess up. That's what people do. But the Lord Jesus Christ is faithful. So just be thankful for what He's doing for you right here and right now...and make the best of it for you and yo kids."

And with that, Money linked arms with his blushing bride, and they exited the room amid thunderous applause.

CHAPTER 26
The Redd Raiders

"Jeb Redd…is that you?"

"Yup," Cousin Jeb whispered, following the caller's lead. "Who's this?"

"This is Essex…Essex LaBrie." He buzzed. "Do you remember me?

"Of course, I remembers ya." Cousin Jeb snickered. "Who can forget a big gun like that?"

"I cannot talk long." Essex pulled him up short. "And I need you to pay close attention. Tout de suite!"

"Okay. Okay." Jeb whined. "What's so gall-darned important?"

"I am very concerned." Essex continued. "I understand Willamina will be in Dallas this weekend—"

"Yeah, and over there at that ACA Awards show on December 14th—Sunday. You know her hit single, 'I Can't Make This Man Love Me,' is up for an award."

"Are you planning to go?"

"No." Jeb slowed. "Hadn't planned to. We was hoping she'd drop down through Houston 'fore she went back to Nashville—"

"I need you to go to Dallas." Essex steamed. "I need you to protect Willamina this weekend."

"Why?" Jeb babbled. "Where you gon' be?"

"I cannot be with Willamina…although it is my greatest desire." Essex admitted. "Since this hit man madness has come up—"

"Hit man?!?"

"I've been keeping a tighter eye on Miz G, and I most assuredly want to be with her in Dallas. But Mizter G will not allow it. He insists that I accompany him to Las Vegas this weekend."

"But—"

"But his request is so out of the ordinary." Essex explained. "He has never…not ever…insisted that I accompany him on a weekend trip where Ryhema…ahh…where his star performer…is in concert."

"O-kay…we knows 'bout that Ryhema gal—"

"And when I requested to be the bodyguard for Miz G in Dallas instead…the mon turned me down flat. Actually, he was furious with me at the suggestion."

"Really?"

"Yes." Essex breathed loudly. "And it got me to thinking that something…something sinister may be up."

"Oh…I see what ya mean," Jeb said wisely. "D-o-u-g don't want ya to protect our sweet, li'l Willamina in Dallas—"

"So I need you and the boys to go to Dallas and look out for Miz G…protect her…all weekend long." Essex's voice tensed. "Is that clear?"

"Sho-nuff." Jeb agreed. "And you can count on us, Essex. We ain't gon' never let Cousin Willamina down."

"Maybe…I am in error." Essex equivocated. "Maybe…everything will work out alright—"

"But it's betta to be safe than sorry…'cause it's gotta work out alright!" Jeb exclaimed. "Or else that ole-boy don't know who he be messing with. Nobody messes over our blood and gets away with it. Nobody!"

"Good. Good." Essex's voice relaxed. "I am in the airport…with Mizter G…so I must go now before he suspects something—"

"Don't worry." Jeb promised. "You can relax yo mind. We's got this!" And before the line went cold, Jeb Redd was rounding up his four other crazy cousins to drive their trucks up to Dallas—convoy style.

When they arrived in Dallas, Jeb and John Earl set up watch in the W Hotel, and the other three made their way to the American Airlines Center where the American Country Awards show was going to be televised. The W Hotel was packed, but Jeb and John Earl squirreled themselves away on the top floor where Willamina had the corner room.

As Jeb suspected, the security was lax and that, too, gave him a queasy feeling in his oversized belly. The laundry room where Jeb and John Earl hid out was pretty much empty since it was the weekend, and the skeleton crew was too excited about the country stars coming to town to pay close attention to their duties. So Jeb and John Earl were taking turns between sleeping in their trucks on the hotel's parking level and the laundry room. They were using the backstairs or the service elevators so they wouldn't get spotted by Cousin Willamina or hotel security.

It was getting late on Sunday night, and Jeb and John Earl were getting hungry. As the weekend had progressed, the cousins had started feeling foolish for hiding out for days in uncomfortable quarters on the word of a near total stranger.

"Cousin Jeb, I'm tired." John Earl whined. "And my belly's grumbling."

"Well, if you think your'n is…whatcha think about mine—"

"Well, you ate the last of the tacos!" John Earl was referring to the sack-full of soft tacos he'd scrounged up from Fuel-up City.

"And boy-howdy they was good!" Jeb sucked his teeth. "Dallas must be the food capital of the world. They're always comin' up with something tasty!"

"We been here all weekend, spying on Willamina and trying not to get caught." John Earl groused. "But what do we really know 'bout this Essex fella?"

"I know we're here on a humbug." Jeb admitted. "But I'd rather us be wrong…than for that fella Essex to be right…and we wasn't here to protect Cousin Willamina—"

"You right, o' course."

"What was that?"

"Don't know." John Earl's glass eye twinkled. "Guess the Awards show is 'bout over and folks is heading back to their rooms."

"Could be." Jeb admitted. "But I'm gonna have a li'l look-see."

When Jeb uncoiled his big body from his hiding place, he peeked out of the laundry room door just in time to see a chalky, white-faced dude, donned in all black from head to toe, creeping down the hallway. "Oh...maybe, he's jes one o' them singer fellas," Jeb buzzed. "Uh-huh, naw, that fella's got a gun in his hand...laid down low on his right thigh." Jeb whispered to John Earl.

"I see what you mean." John Earl peeked around him at the door.

"That don't look right," Jeb said.

"Naw." John Earl agreed. "'Specially since he's a tryna break into Willamina's room right this minute—"

"Let's git him!" Cousin Jeb slid through the door and John Earl was on his heels.

Before the gunman could swing around from Willamina's door, John Earl had lassoed him with a knotted rope and drug him down the corridor like a twisting bale of hay. Had they taken noticed, Jeb and John R. would've gotten a hoot out of the total look of astonishment on the trapped man's face. But instead, Cousin Jeb clobbered him in the head with the butt of his shotgun and pocketed the hit man's big, black pistol that had skidded across the floor.

"Now, what we do with him?" John Earl panted.

"We gon' git him outta this hallway 'fore anybody else shows up...'specially Willamina—"

"Let's take him down to the parking level where we's got our trucks at."

"Yep." Cousin Jeb hiccupped loudly, putting on his best drunk act. "We'll just let everybody think we's had ourselves a li'l too much to drink." They lifted up the man by his shoulders and staggered toward the service elevators.

When they got to the parking level, Jeb searched the man's pockets. He removed his extra bullet clips, a wad of cash, a picture of Willamina taken in front of her home in Nashville, and the key-card to her hotel suite. "No wallet."

"Guess he don't want nobody to know his name."

"Guess not." Jeb snickered. "Well, no never-mind; he won't be needing it no mo'."

"Should I call the boys?" John Earl offered when they'd made it to the truck.

"You bet." Cousin Jeb forced a black bag over the gunman's head—the one they'd brought with them for just such an occasion—and zip-tied it. They threw John R. from NOLA into the back of the truck. "Tell the boys to meet us up in them-thar hills." Cousin Jeb squeezed out a blood-tingling wolf howl. "Whoo-Whoo-Whoo!"

CHAPTER 27
The Redd Revenge

The second Board meeting of Star Music Promotions International, Inc., held in the Grand Boardroom of the Waldorf Astoria Hotel in Nashville, was called to order precisely at 2 p.m. by Chairman Douglas Grand on Tuesday, December 16th. The massive board table was set-up in its usual order: Douglas Grand at the helm; Willamina Redd-Grand at his right hand; corporate lawyer, Jim Jenkins, at his left; and his nine yes-men filled the remaining chairs. The stockholders in attendance were stationed around the walls in side chairs.

When Willamina had walked into the room five minutes before the call to order, Douglas' eyes had bloomed into vacant, white orbs. He hadn't heard from John R. directly, but when his wife had missed her return flight and failed to return home from Dallas on Monday, he was sure the deed had been done. He didn't know how John R. planned to do it, but her body was not to be found until after the Board meeting. In fact, Douglas had forged Willamina's signature and was planning to vote her shares by proxy. He was anxiously awaiting instructions from John R. for making the second half of the payment for the $25,000 job. *A small price to pay to get my business straight.*

Willamina, on the other hand, was totally unaware of her cousins' visit to Dallas the previous weekend, or the shenanigans that had gone on in her hallway on Sunday night. But just out of the blue on Monday, she'd decided to drive from Dallas to Nashville instead of flying because she wanted to have a long talk with her broker along the way. On her drive, she had let Douglas' repeated calls to her cellphone go unanswered. She didn't want to talk to him. She wanted to spit in his eye at the Board meeting.

When she'd arrived in Nashville in the wee hours of Tuesday morning, Willamina had avoided going home to Douglas. Instead, she'd grabbed a nap in one of the hotel rooms upstairs before it was time for the Board meeting. Essex's heart had literally skipped a beat when he saw her exit the elevator on the Boardroom floor, and he was proud to escort her into the meeting moments before the gavel sounded.

"Good morning, Willamina" was all that Douglas could squawk out as she took her rightful place at the table. "Congrats on your ACA for Best Single. You look radiant. Uhh…when did you get back?"

"Good morning, yo'self, Douglas," Willamina replied coolly. "And that's more than I can say for you. You look rode-hard-and-put-up-wet."

With that, Douglas landed his gavel and called the meeting to order.

"Mr. Chairman." Willamina flung back her long red locks and cleared her throat. She was dressed to the nines in all black—from her calf-skin blazer to her eel-skin boots. It made for a startling contrast against her lily-white skin and minimal makeup. "I request that since we have a number of stockholders in attendance today." She smiled and nodded at the growing audience. "I request that we have a voice vote on our agenda items." She was all business. *It's about time Douglas Grand gets to know who I am…I'm a mountain woman!*

"A voice vote?" Douglas was taken off guard by Willamina's presence. In fact, he plastered her face with question marks because he couldn't fathom how it was she'd survived John R.'s attack; and how it was she was still alive and able to make the meeting. But in the oft chance she was still voting his way, Douglas endeavored to be polite. "Is a voice vote in order?" Douglas said, turning to Jim Jenkins, the corporate lawyer sitting to his left.

"Yes, sir, Mr. Chairman," Jenkins spoke up crisply. "A voice vote is in order for these proceedings. And to those of you present, we are recording these proceedings on three microphones posted around the room, so please speak up clearly and concisely when it becomes your turn to vote. These recordings will be used to prepare the final minutes of the meeting."

"Very well." Douglas consented.

"And in the interest of time, Mr. Chairman," the lawyer continued, "I suggest we proceed with the Nay votes first."

"Very well." Douglas pulled back on the reins. "Item 1 on the agenda under New Business," he said clearly. "A change to our charter and company name to include the word 'Distribution' e.g. Star Music Promotions/Distribution International, Inc., for the purpose of acquiring Hickock Global Distribution, a family owned company." Douglas looked over and smiled at Willamina to test the waters, and she smiled back. "The Chair will entertain the Nay votes at this time."

"One shareholder from Rhode Island stood and said, "Mr. Chairman, I represent less than one percent of the voting shares, and I vote Nay."

Then Cousin Jeb stood. Douglas had spotted him and his band of crazy cousins out of the corner of his eye before the meeting began, but he'd given their presence not the least bit of credence. "Mr. Chairman, D-O-U-G." Jeb spoke up clearly and concisely. "The five of us vote Nay." He pointed to his four side-kicks. "And we represent *15%* of the voting shares—"

Douglas' jaw dropped.

"Not hide-nor-hair." Cousin Jeb continued; his eyes squinted like daggers in Douglas' direction. *"Not hide-nor-hair."* He repeated firmly.

"Your comments are out of order, sir." The lawyer spoke up, but Douglas understood fully what he meant. John R., his faithful hit

152

man, was somewhere up in *them-thar hills*, never to be seen or heard of again. Willamina eyed Cousin Jeb, totally perplexed, but her family would see to it and her peace of mind that she never knew the evil fate Douglas had planned for her.

While Cousin Jeb had been speaking, Wanza and Money Mann were permitted into the room by Essex, who was holding sentry at the door and checking shareholder credentials. Essex smiled at finally making the acquaintance of the infamous, newlywed Money Mann. But he also had his Sig Sauer tucked away, just in case there was any unnecessary ruckus.

Money stood and said, "Mr. Chairman, my wife and I, Mrs. Wanza Johnson-Mann, vote Nay, and we represent *5%* of the voting shares." And as he took his seat he added, "And this one, *D-O-U-G*, is for Missy!"

Douglas was stunned. He felt like he'd been sucker punched. And as he tallied it, the Nays accounted for over 20%. Things were getting too close for comfort. He cleared his voice and said, "The Chairman is making a last call for Nay votes—"

Willamina, who was seated at his right, raised her hand. "Mr. Chairman," she said clearly, "I vote Nay, and I represent *31%* of the voting shares—"

"No, you do not!" Douglas blasted. "You represent only *21%* at best—"

"Check with your lawyer, there." Willamina calmly held her ground. "He has the proper documentation."

Douglas' neck snapped so hard to the left that it made a crackling sound in the noiseless room. "Is what she said true?" He sprayed the lawyer with his hot saliva. Unbeknownst to Douglas, when he'd encouraged Essex to make a play for Willamina by telling him they had an open marriage, her first call had been to her broker. At that point, she started buying up as many extra shares as she could get her hands on—31% to be exact. And her last calls to her broker, on her drive in route to Nashville, confirmed for her that her mission had been accomplished, and the corporate lawyer had been notified. It had cost her millions, but she thought it well-worth the investment. Meanwhile, she'd gifted her original 21% to her family and friends—the ones who'd been devastated by Douglas' trickery, lies and raw ambition—and she'd invited them to attend the Board meeting, as well.

"Yes, Mr. Chairman." The lawyer checked his most recent paperwork. "That is correct. Mrs. Willamina Redd-Grand does indeed represent 31% of the voting shares."

"What?" Douglas was counting on his fingers and toes trying to come up with enough Yea votes to have his way. But even with his 30% share, Willamina's 31%, along with the 20% from her cronies, gave her the decided 51% majority. Not in a million years, would he have thought *Pretty Miss Redd* capable of such expert maneuvering. Blinded by pride and eager obsession, he'd judged her wrongly. He'd failed to get to know his people, and he had absolutely no idea what his hillbilly bride and her goat-roper clan were capable of.

"Mr. Chairman." The lawyer called it. "The Nays have it. The proposal to change the corporate charter, corporate name and acquire Hickock Global Distribution, a family owned company, is defeated."

"Whoosh—" The air blew out of Douglas' deflated pride with a noise. The look on his crestfallen face was almost palpable. Everyone in the room could see that this was a Kodak moment for the *agony of defeat*. Douglas was almost unable to continue.

But in the silence, Willamina's voice rose like a phoenix. "Mr. Chairman," she said, "I would like to add an item of New Business—"

"Impossible!" Douglas rebounded. "The agenda is set!" He protested. "No new items can be added at this late date—"

"I beg to differ, sir," Willamina said politely. "Our bylaws clearly state that a Vote of Confidence for any member of the Board can be added to the agenda at any time—"

"Wha—?" Douglas gasped, turning to the lawyer.

"That's correct, Mr. Chairman." The lawyer parroted, eyes wide with amazement. *What is Douglas' wife up to? This is highly irregular!*

"In that case, Mr. Chairman," Willamina said unswervingly, "I call to a vote the position of Chairman of the Board and Chief Executive Officer—"

The buzz was so loud in the room that no one heard the lawyer banging on the table to regain control. Essex ducked his head in from his post, pistol in hand, to be sure everyone was safe and sound.

"Chairman of the Board?" The lawyer clarified as soon as order was restored.

"Yes, sir." Willamina held firm. "Chairman of the Board and Chief Executive Officer."

Douglas was too flabbergasted to speak. He looked as if he'd been transformed into a block of stone. But under the circumstances, the lawyer couldn't allow him to speak. Douglas could not be allowed to carry the vote for his own position.

"We will entertain a voice vote," the lawyer said plainly. "All in favor of Mr. Douglas Grand stepping down as Chairman/CEO of Star Music Promotions International, Incorporated stand and voice your votes." He raised his hand to continue. "We will entertain the Nay votes first." After all the Nay votes were voiced and recorded, the lawyer asked for the Yea votes.

The room ripped open like an avalanche. Cousin Jeb spoke first. Wanza and Money went next. And in all the ruckus, no one noticed when another slinky stockholder slid into the room.

"Sir, I vote Yea." A sultry voice arose from the back of the room. It was Ryhema, and she was standing there with a man named Cosmos. "And I represent *1%* of the voting shares," she said, icicles dripping. "*D-o-u-g*, you've messed over one woman too many."

Willamina had made her move—check and mate. Of her original 21%, she'd given 15% to her five cousins; 5% as a wedding present to Money and Wanza; and 1% to Ryhema, so they could be there to see Douglas get his due. His precious empire—the one he'd built on all of their backs—was ready to crash and burn, and she wanted them to have the chance to participate.

Willamina had couriered the documents to Ryhema with a sweet note, inviting her to attend the Board meeting and voice her vote, if she were so inclined. Ryhema had quickly responded and vowed to attend if her pain was gone. The wink she gave Willamina after her vote was proof that it had. Willamina had been certain that her family and the Manns would vote her way; but in order to insure herself the 51% majority, she had bought 31% for herself—not just 30%—just in case Ryhema had a change of heart. Willamina fastened her arms across her beautiful bosom in tight resolve. *Always keep a spare...that's what a mountain woman would do.*

With Ryhema's abdication from his camp, Douglas looked like a heavyweight boxer who'd been given the standing ten-count. He saw that she'd removed his *Rock of Gibraltar* from her left ring finger, and he knew all hope was lost; he couldn't bully her into staying by his side any longer. His eyes glazed over. He would've missed the next jolt entirely if the messenger hadn't made such a floor-show of an entrance.

As the lawyer was calling out, "The Yeas have it with 52% of the voting shares, a young man with a bad haircut and tight jeans burst into the room. He'd been admitted with Essex's permission, of course. "Which one of you is Douglas Grand?" The young man yelled.

Douglas didn't move. He couldn't. His address was in another hemisphere. Absently, the lawyer pointed to Douglas, and the young process server squeezed a summons into his clammy palm. "You've been served!" he yelled and made a swift exit.

Douglas was catatonic, so the lawyer removed the summons from his groping fingers. And he was so stunned, he read it aloud: Bill of Divorcement from Complainant, Willamina Redd-Grand to Plaintiff, Douglas Grand."

That was it! The whole room fainted. Only Willamina and the lawyer were able to have a sane discourse. "Does this mean you're filing for divorce from Mr. Grand?" The lawyer stated the obvious.

"It does." Willamina didn't blink an eye.

"On what grounds, may I ask?" The lawyer was dumbfounded.

"On the grounds that he violated our prenup—"

"Huh?" The word prenup had brought Douglas out of La-La Land for a moment of cogent thought.

"Yes," Willamina said, looking Douglas squarely in his eyes. She lowered her voice to a quiet snarl that only he and his lawyer could hear. "You cheated on me with Ryhema in violation of the prenup that you crafted. And as such, you owe me one-half of *all* your worldly goods—"

"Wha—?" The word cracked from Douglas' tortured face.

"Wha—?" The lawyer staggered.

"I didn't bring it up earlier." Willamina continued. "But the 30% voting shares that you used today…actually…they belong to me." *Now, ain't that better than a skillet upside his head, Grandma Betsy?*

"Wha—?" Douglas fainted.

"Wha—?" The lawyer fainted.

"And there being no further business on the agenda," one of the brave stockholder's said, "I move that Ms. Willamina Redd be appointed as Acting Chairman and CEO of Star Music Promotions

International, Inc. until such time as a suitable replacement can be recruited and hired."

"Second the Motion."

"Yea!" The entire room screamed, absent a peep out of Douglas and his lawyer.

"As Acting Chairman," Willamina said, stepping right into her new role. "I will now entertain a Motion for Adjournment."

"So moved!"

"Meeting adjourned."

Quickly, Essex ushered in the paramedics he'd called to attend to a stupefied Douglas Grand and his lawyer.

EPILOGUE

The Grand Finale

Douglas was a wreck. He was stinky, wretched and stubbly. He hadn't shaved and showered for days, and his smooth, dark, handsome face was being overtaken by a five-day-old beard. His living space was cluttered with half-eaten pizza, Chinese food containers, empty liquor bottles and beer mugs. He was subsisting on fast food deliveries because he was too ashamed to be seen in public.

Books, papers and old records were strewn all over his shiny hardwood floors. Douglas had haggled with his fleet of lawyers and accountants until the final verdict was in. He'd lost everything. His precious brainchild, Star Music Promotions International, Inc. was out of his control; and his personal fortune had gone down the tubes with his failed takeover of Hickock Global Distribution. And what the Hickock deal hadn't cost him, Willamina Redd would soak up through her divorce proceedings. *That blasted prenup!*

In fact, Douglas' lawyers and accountants had started to refuse his calls, simply because they knew he could no longer afford to pay their exorbitant billable hours. The staff at Star had turned inward. With Willamina acting as Chairman/CEO, holding onto their jobs required giving her and the company their complete loyalty. Even Chad, his faithful, long-time assistant, had taken great pleasure in turning his back on Douglas. Without a moment's hesitation, he'd clued Willamina in on Douglas' would-be, hush-hush numbered account stashed away in the Cayman Islands. But like any good assistant, Chad knew where all the bones were buried.

As soon as the Board of Directors' meeting had ended, Willamina had thrown Douglas out of her prestigious penthouse in Opryland Towers. And since his mansion on Legend's Way hadn't sold yet—the mansion he'd shared with Melissa—he was forced to move back into it. The furnishings were still intact so that the realtors could show it off, but the walls of priceless art works, which had been carefully selected by Melissa, had long since been sold off to the highest bidder. Douglas had lost everything he dearly loved. And as he wandered the empty halls of the house muttering to himself like a wounded ghost, he was beginning to think he was also losing his mind.

"What's left for me?" Douglas grumbled to himself. "I'm broke...busted...tapped out! I don't own one single, solitary thing, except this house...that I hate...my Rolls...and the clothes on my back. Willamina took all of my stock that was worth anything, and what the Hickock deal didn't rob from me, she did. *Heartless Vampire*! Douglas crumbled to the couch with his head in his hands. "And now...I'm too old...too tired...to start all over again...from scratch? Never! What am I supposed to do...sell bootleg CDs outta the trunk of my Rolls? Impossible!"

"I have nothing...and no one. I never had any friends...never needed any. I've always been a lion in a world full of sheep. Men feared me." Douglas slugged back the remains of a warm beer. "But Pastor Meadows warned me...preached at me...about leaving these crazy, vindictive women alone...and look at me now. They used me! They used me up!"

Douglas howled a wicked laugh. "And it all started with Wanza. She was my Ace. But it was her fault she didn't keep pace. She wouldn't step-up her game...and she knew I couldn't have that. And my boys...my poor boys...they don't even know me...or care." He flung the empty beer bottle, and it shattered against the wall.

"And Melissa," he spat out her name, "*Sweet-Little-Innocent Melissa*...she was a first-class leach. All she wanted were the things a rich man could buy her. She wanted to be Mrs. Douglas Grand...and she did anything to get her wish. But where was she when I needed her? Ha!" Douglas slugged down the remaining corner from one of the liquor bottles.

"And worst of all...worst of all...I lost the only woman I have ever really loved. She stole my ring and my heart! *Ravishing Ryhema!*" He screamed out loud. "And to lose her to an impotent nothing...a useless crumb like Cosmos! Grrrrr!"

Douglas' wretched growls soon turned into the burning tears of a drunk and desperate man. "Look at all my marriage to Willamina has cost me...her and her crazy pack of hillbilly bumpkins. How could I have known what a family like that was capable of? *That's the problem with marriage...you never know who you're dealing with... until it's too late!* And Essex; after all I did for him, the worm turned on me when I needed him the most. I just know he had something to do with undermining my plans with John R." Douglas drained the bottle.

"And Wanza and Money...married! Really?!? Money Mann... Melissa's jail-bird brother...married to my Wanza?!? And Wanza and Money...together...there to see me fall...to team-up on me...to vote against me...to laugh at me to my face...to witness my darkest hour! They've all probably been plotting against me this whole time. All of 'em! And the thought of Money Mann...around my little boys...that ex-felon...that loser!"

"WHAT-THE-WHAT?!?" Douglas' paranoia seared through his gut like a white-hot poker. "How could they? After all I did for them? All of 'em! How could they...turn against me...betray me? I hate 'em! I hate 'em...I hate 'em...ALL!

Douglas stumbled up from the couch and kicked at the debris that was mounting around his feet. "My life is over...over!" He slurred. "Ole Money should o' just put a bullet in my head at True Vine. Humph! And since he didn't, I guess it's up to me to finish the job."

He staggered into his home office, landing hard against his custom-made mahogany desk. He unlocked the bottom drawer and rummaged around until his hand fell upon his automatic pistol. Gun in hand, Douglas flopped into his high-back leather chair, cradling the lethal weapon like a baby. He wiped the tears and sweat from his eyes and checked to see if the gun was loaded.

"I'm sorry, Melissa!" Douglas cried out loud in a drunken stupor and fell down to his knees. "I…am…truly…sorry!" He placed the gun at his right temple and cocked it. The sound of the hammer readying itself for action was deafening in the quiet room. Douglas placed his finger on the trigger. But at that very moment, his telephone rang. Would he ever know it was his old friend, Pastor Meadows, reaching out to bring him comfort?

****

"Lo, this is the man that made not God his strength;
but trusted in the abundance of his riches,
and strengthened himself in his wickedness."
~Psalm 52:7

Other Books by the Author
JEANETTA BRITT

Exciting Novels

The Fire Series:
    Dipped in the Fire (Book 1)   (ISBN 978-0-6923005-0-3)
    Double-Dipped in the Fire (Book 2) (ISBN 978-1-7327071-0-8)
*Living in the Seventh Day   (ISBN 978-0-6923005-0-3)
*W.O.O.F. (Women of Overcoming Faith) (ISBN 978-0-9712363-8-7)
*Empty Envelope   (ISBN 978-0-9712363-5-6)
The Lottie Series:
    Pickin' Ground (Book 1)   (ISBN 0-9712363-3-x)
    In Due Season (Book 2)   (ISBN 0-9712363-4-8)
    Lottie (Book 3)   (ISBN 0-9712363-6-4)

[E-Books also available!]

Inspiring Poetry

*The Collection—Poems of Praise *(ebook only)*
*Flittin' & Flyin'   (ISBN 978-0-9712363-9-4)
*Under the Influence—Spoken Praise (ISBN 0-9712363-7-2)
The Trilogy:
    Poems from the Fast   (ISBN 0-9712363-0-5)
    Reunion   (ISBN 0-9712363-1-3)
    Third Ear   (ISBN 0-9712363-2-1)

Join Jeanetta online:
www.jbrittbooks.com
www.Facebok.com/JBrittBooks
www.Twitter.com/@JBrittBooks
www.Amazon.com/Jeanetta Britt
www.bn.com/Jeanetta Britt

ABOUT THE AUTHOR

Jeanetta Britt is a bestselling author who graduated with honors from Fisk University and The University of Michigan. Her passion for writing contemporary Christian Fiction novels—filled with lots of juicy drama and suspense—as well as, Gospel poetry, surfaced in 1996 and has grown steadily since that time. "While being swept up in the story," Jeanetta says, "I want my readers to *feel* the love of Jesus and take refuge in Him, like I did."

After completing a rewarding career in public administration in Dallas, Texas, Jeanetta returned to her native Alabama to write and to live. Her southern roots are reflected in her strong imagery, memorable characters, and delightfully witty storytelling style. She is a sought-after inspirational speaker, by youth and adults alike, with eight novels and six books of poetry to her credit.

Jeanetta is also an avid gardener and community advocate, and she founded Twelve Stones CDC—a non-profit organization that operates two community gardens in rural Alabama. "We provide free, fresh food for our community and an opportunity for our youth and senior citizens to form vital intergenerational connections, and to get some free exercise, companionship and sunshine, too," she says. "No rules—just love!"

www.ingramcontent.com/pod-product-compliance
Lightning Source LLC
Chambersburg PA
CBHW060747180626
46818CB00002B/482